The Killing of Ros Grenham

Michael G. Casey

ISBN 978-1-9160264-2-1

First edition, 2019

Published by Azimuth Publishing
Dublin, Ireland

Photographic images used in the cover (all are altered from
the originals) courtesy of psyberartist, Mark Fisher, and
Peter Brown, all via Flickr.

Layout, cover design by iCulture

Please visit michaelgcasey.com

ABOUT THIS BOOK

Niall Grenham, a 'failed priest', emigrated to the US. He married Rona and they had a daughter, Ros, who is the light of their lives. Ros grows up to be an accomplished and well-meaning young woman. Niall cannot credit his good fortune.

After a late-night graduation party, Ros tries to help her childhood friend, Mark, who has gone off the rails and is addicted to drugs. Motivated by jealousy, he engineers a car accident in which Ros is brutally killed.

Mark's father, who works in the British Embassy, Washington D.C., is the first to realise what has happened. He puts Mark on a plane to New York to alibi him.

Niall and Rona try to deal with their grievous loss in different ways, which causes some estrangement between them. When Niall discovers it was not an accident, and there is not enough evidence to bring Mark to trial, he begins a kind of psychological warfare against Mark and his father. He gives Mark money for drugs, and gives him souvenirs of his early life with Ros. He shows him home movies that feature them both as children, happily playing. He feels diminished by these tactics but will not quit.

After many months, the pressure exerted by Niall produces a result, but does it make any difference to his monumental sense of loss? He follows Mark and his father to another country and is prepared to put his own life, marriage, and faith on the line for the sake of his beloved daughter, Ros.

"Bad things, as we know, can happen to good people. But what choices do they make when justice turns away? We live the pain of the bereaved father, and we struggle with the rightness of his decisions. This is compelling writing, in which we feel dilemmas we hope never to confront."
—Peter FitzGerald

BOOKS PREVIOUSLY PUBLISHED
BY MICHAEL G. CASEY

Come Home, Robbie, a novel, published by The O'Brien Press, 1990

> "…page-turning urgency … spine-tingling compulsion … the sheer quality of the writing lends the story some of the stature of heroic tragedy."
> —The Education Times

Treadmill, an award-winning Chapbook of short stories, published by Tipperary Arts Centre and Start Magazine, 2008

> "…Casey brings to life vivid characters who captivate, amuse and engage … (He) has a wry observation and quick wit."
> —Mike McCormack

Ireland's Malaise: The Troubled Personality of the Irish Economy, published by The Liffey Press, 2010

> "…(Casey) shows the same Confucian wisdom as his hero, T.K. Whitaker in his brilliant new book."

—Eoghan Harris, The Sunday Independent

The Visit, a novel, published by The Anaphora Press, 2011

> "…a small Irish town deals with a major event … an interesting addition to the genre … clear-eyed … vivid description…"
> —Denis Fahey, Historian

> "…a lovely clear prose style … some great characters and beautifully crafted vignettes."
> —Stella Kane, Quartet Books Ltd

Broken Circle, a collection of poetry, due to be published by Salmon Press in Spring 2019

> "…very powerful, intelligent poems made their presence known immediately … (Casey) uses casuistry and persuasiveness to rival Robert Browning's dramatic Monologues…"
> —Derek Selen

DEDICATION

For: Saoirse, Orlagh, Cian, Isabella and Darren.

PART I

CHAPTER 1

ROS GRENHAM RUMMAGED in her purse for the car keys. The family pet, a spaniel called Hamm, bounded to help and was rewarded by a pat on the head and a tickle under the chin. Ros was his favourite family member because, in recognition of his advancing years, she often slipped him special treats. Every bit of him quivered and cavorted as if he sensed a great event in the offing. As Ros did a final check of her purse, in preparation for her graduation party, her parents looked on in bewilderment. How on earth had the tiny, wrinkled infant they'd brought home from the maternity hospital some twenty-one years ago turned into this accomplished and elegant young woman?

Her father, Niall, unable to break the habit of a lifetime, issued all sorts of dire warnings about the hazards of 'going out'.

"Don't worry, Dad." Ros smiled. "I'm all grown up now. I'll probably stay at Gillian's house tonight." She waved and then blew them a kiss.

Rona, her Mom, asked her to submit her face for inspection in case Hamm had done damage to her make-up. Niall advised his wife to cease and desist since his daughter didn't wear make-up and never had.

"Well, I do, a little, Dad. I'm not Amish."

"You don't need to wear any."

Rona completed the inspection. "OK, Ros, have fun." She settled back into a flower-patterned armchair.

"Take care," Niall added as Ros skipped down the steps towards her car. The screen door slammed shut after her, keeping out the fireflies and gnats that enlivened the warm dusk.

"She worked hard," Niall remarked, as if he had to justify all forms of enjoyment. But everything had come relatively easy to Ros, he reflected. She could study standing on her head with the TV blaring and Hamm barking for attention. Wonderful powers of concentration – and poise. No, more than that. Grace. She was blessed, a blessed daughter. The world was now her oyster and the thought of her working in some other country scared him rigid. He couldn't let go and he knew it.

"A pity about Mark flunking out." Rona dented out an awkward fold in *The Washington Post.*

"There's a lack in that boy," Niall mused. "It's not just the damned drugs. Diplomats' kids get dragged around the globe. It can't have been easy for him." Mark and Ros had been good friends once, especially in their early teens. It was strange how they had veered off in separate directions, as if answering different drumbeats. Just as well for Ros though. She had tried her best to help him, but he threw her attempts back in her face, as he gradually became dependent on drugs, prescription drugs in the first instance.

"Oh, you Europeans," Rona sniffed. "You don't know the meaning of mobility. I'd lived in five different states before I was fifteen."

"The same country though," Niall pointed out. Though was it the same? The diversity of America amazed him – people, cultures, geography. He stretched out his legs and scanned the headlines of the newspaper which Rona held in front of her. As usual she turned the page just when he was getting interested in an item. Another Senator had fetched up in jail. Open government was coming of age, or was it? He imagined there were degrees of transparency.

The party was quieter than Ros had expected. All of the ingredients were there – good music, food and drink, people dancing – but something was lacking. She and her classmates seemed to sense that an era was over and that they would shortly be going their separate ways. Her best friend, Gillian, had already accepted a job offer in Germany, where there was still a demand for engineers. She sat with her for a while, sipping punch, but each knew that their chat was a prelude to farewells. They knew they'd meet up again on special occasions but there was no escaping the mood of separation that overlay them. When Gillian got up to dance, Ros went out to the small balcony of the brownstone house and looked for a while at the few stars that shone through the cloud cover.

She was joined by Mark Highsmith. He had obviously been drinking and it seemed likely from his pinned eyes that he had taken something else as well. She was sorry for him in a way and could sense how left out he felt. Of course it was his own fault; he had done little or no study even in the final term. Still... She shrugged off his clumsy advances but he continued to paw her.

"Stop it, Mark. Please stop."

"Come on, Ros ... We used to be pals." He lunged at her. She could have stepped aside but was afraid that he might fall over the balustrade. Although they were only two floors up he could be badly injured, if not worse. She stood her ground and pushed him backwards.

"Friends, yes. Now cut it out." As neighbours, they had more or less grown up together and she was upset to see him behaving like this.

"You're turning ... into a little tease." He swayed and tried to focus on her face, which was half in shadow.

"If you say so." There was no point in arguing with him. Besides, she wasn't in any real danger.

"Success isn't all it's cracked up to be ... Look at all those fucking nerds back in there." He jerked his thumb over his shoulder.

"Why don't you sort yourself out, Mark?"

She had a sudden vivid recollection of a group of them playing on the swing-set in her back yard when they were about six or seven. Gillian asked him where his Mom was. He began to answer but tears came to his eyes and he turned away. After that Ros looked out for him as best she could but he came to reject her kindness. She still found it hard to believe that he had turned out the way he did but she hoped he could take charge of his life before it was too late. Her serious tone held him at bay for a while.

"I'm OK," he slurred. "Don't worry about me. There has to be one or two bullshit artists. Statistically, we have to exist. Get it? I'm like Jesus … taking all your sins, on my shoulders. You owe me … for that." He grabbed her by the arm and tried to kiss her. She broke free and went back indoors through the French windows.

Shortly afterwards she left the party which was dying on its feet. Gillian had already left with her boyfriend, but Ros had a key to her house in Langley. As she drove over Key Bridge towards Virginia she noticed the lights of a jeep in her rearview mirror. The jeep was being driven erratically, wandering all over the road, coming up close behind her then dropping back. It had to be Mark; she pulled over to the hard shoulder and got out.

"For god's sake, Mark, you shouldn't be driving in your state," she said through the half-open window of the jeep.

"Concerned are we?" The expression on his

face mocked her but there was self-loathing in it too. The cocktail of dex and barbs was having its effect. "Don't give me that shit."

"Leave the jeep there. I'll drive you home if you promise to…"

"I'll promise nothing … you tight-ass. Just because you got your exams … you think you're somethin' special…"

"Come on, get in the car."

He leant out of the window and pushed her away. "Leave me alone … just fuck off ."

"Well, follow me then. I'll go by your house first. And take it easy." She got back into the car and pulled out into the slow lane. There was virtually no traffic at that hour and she felt that with a little luck he would make it all right. Just past the next bend she was suddenly dazzled by his lights. They were on full beam, and he was much too close. She tried to accelerate but the first sickening impact made her lose control of the wheel. The second collision snapped her head back. Then forwards as her car hit the wall above the Potomac. Shocked and badly hurt she tried to remain conscious. It was her only hope. She tried to reverse but could not locate the gear-shift. When she did, her wheels began to spin. The lights of the jeep bore down on her. She began to pass out. He rammed the back of her car again and this time her head hit the roof, breaking her neck. The next assault sent her car through the wall. It careered down the slope towards the river, coming to rest at a tulip tree startlingly in flower. Mark got out expecting to see an explosion. There was none. The car slid gently into the river and the water closed over it. Planes heading for Reagan Airport were stacked overhead, their lights reflected in the river. Mark staggered back towards the jeep...

CHAPTER 2

EARLIER THAT DAY Mark's father, David Highsmith, put in his usual few hours in the embassy. He had long since arrived at the conclusion that his work was of no importance. At best it was reportage, a form of lower-order intelligence. He delegated as much as he could to his new First Secretary – a young woman who was as keen as mustard. He looked over her draft report on the US Budget, wincing at the appalling escalator prose – spending up, taxes down, borrowing up, etc. Why on earth was Whitehall interested in this stuff anyway? It would be in the Financial Times the next day. Maybe the lead time of a few hours was important to the mandarins for whom being first in the know was a merit badge or a consolation prize for the loss of empire.

In a way though, the job suited him. After his wife's death – in a drowning accident in India, his last posting – he didn't need any challenges in his life. His problem son was enough. Washington met his material needs quite well. In the sixties it was regarded as a hardship post but now in the late noughties the city had come of age and, in terms of the ordinary comforts of life, had an edge over London.

Because David had no ambitions and made no secret of his contempt for the job, his colleagues tended to treat him with respect. He would frequently leave the office early to get back to his comfortable home to swim in the pool or read and sip martinis. As a widower he wasn't expected to do much entertaining at home, which was just as well since standing around at receptions gave him a severe headache and pains in his calf muscles. Besides, his tolerance for diplomatic chatter had hit rock bottom.

There was a woman, Julie Kinch, whom he met about twice a week at lunchtime. *L'amour d'après-midi* – or 'nooners' as the indigenes called it – was one of the institutional features of Washington which he liked best. All of the hotels around the Pentagon did a roaring trade in renting rooms to the top brass on an hourly basis between noon and three p.m. There was a cluster of hotels near the Capitol which catered for politicians and another cluster near Embassy Row. It was to one of these hotels that David made his way in a taxi.

Julie was waiting for him when he arrived. She wore her dark hair in a twist that went down to the small of her back, and she carried herself well; there was more than a hint of the catwalk in her bearing. David had been a little put off initially by the commercial nature of the transaction but gradually he came to appreciate the mediation of the almighty buck which eliminated coyness, moods, sulky withdrawal of favours, vaginal wrench, headaches and so on. This was the American way, efficient, explicit –

and they managed to have considerable fun.

She moved towards him and helped him off with his jacket, then his shirt. These were laid carefully on the back of a chair in case he might have to go back to the office. It was a minor miracle every time – and refreshingly straightforward. It was one of the accommodations that DC offered to the hard-pressed executive or senior bureaucrat. And if Julie didn't enjoy it too, she was a damned good actress. He sometimes saw himself as a poisonous snake having its venom extracted, and occasionally wondered if that was also how Julie saw it as she worked her magic. He had even become used to the female condom which he had initially described as a Wellington boot – although a hoover bag was probably closer to the mark. Julie had somehow managed to invest that crass device with a little fun. Only in America… Though later on they settled for the traditional condom, often provided by her when he forgot.

With her, reality was better than fantasy. She invariably sent him away a little less ornery, a little more inclined to believe there might be some good in the world – until the venom built up again in his veins.

Dressing afterwards was part of the ritual, diminished only by the thought that he would have to put in another hour or so in the embassy in the afternoon.

"Do you have to go back?" she asked with a pouty expression.

"'Fraid so." He stood like a schoolboy while she brushed some lint from the shoulder of his jacket and straightened his tie. Such a wifely touch seemed out of place. There was no question of handing her a bundle of notes. He paid her discreetly at the end of each month by leaving a cheque in one of her high-heel shoes.

"See you on Wednesday?"

"Wouldn't miss it," she lilted.

Although a partner in the firm, Niall had spent the early part of a morning some days previously on one of the building sites to supervise the delivery of prefab roof sections. The hard hat, which was a size too big, rested on his rather prominent ears. As he chatted with the foreman, he noticed how the workers had to make frequent trips to the drinks machine. He wondered how they could do that heavy work in such deadening heat. The crane driver sat aloft in a sweltering glass cab barely visible in the haze. Niall marvelled at their resilience, and envied it. He himself couldn't even play golf in this humidity.

"I see the ads for this lot are in the property pages already," the foreman observed. "What's the response like?"

"We've had a good few inquiries," Niall answered. "Sold a couple of units from the drawings. I think demand is picking up." It had occurred to him that one of these town houses would be perfect for Ros, assuming her first job didn't take her away from the area.

The thought of being able to visit her regularly filled him with hope. He liked being near her, in the same room. They didn't have to talk much; the odd comment was enough. Her presence was what mattered; as long as she was there he didn't want to be anywhere else. A hundred-plus TV channels were no substitute whenever she left the room. And it must have been obvious too because his amused spouse sometimes told him to get a life.

"Well, they tell us the recession is nearly over."

"Looks like it. At least until the Fed jacks up interest rates." By adding that glum caveat it occurred to Niall that he was beginning to sound like old Laughlin, his senior partner – not a pleasant thought. Although Laughlin was due to retire in less than a year and Niall would have an opportunity to buy the firm, he wasn't entirely comfortable with the prospect of being number one. Rona would have to stiffen his resolve; indeed, she had already begun to drop little hints. He watched the crane lower the roof units into place and the workmen bolt them down. Watching the buildings take shape always filled him with awe. Maybe his two years of philosophy made him a sucker for concrete things. He could never understand how they got the measurements so right, so perfect. Doing his job was a doddle by comparison. And of course the realtors and lawyers made big bucks by doing very little, apart from lunching, making contacts, and flapping their gums. He was glad Ros had chosen to do engineering; she would make a contribution, achieve something tangible.

It was now, what, twenty-five years since he decided the priesthood was not for him and went through the agonising process of exclaustration – the first step towards laicisation. He left the seminary on a cold March morning in a second-hand suit of clothes, carrying a tin of instant coffee and a reading lamp. He watched the grey monolith of Maynooth recede behind him and as it vanished from sight the only sense of security he'd ever experienced went with it. To this day he could remember the cold fear that crawled through his stomach as he boarded the bus for Dublin. He was convinced that he had blown his only hope of a fulfilling (and safe) life. His wily old father used to say: 'You only get one chance, boy, and you're lucky if you get that much.' How wrong he was.

In less than a decade Niall had landed a job in the States, met and married Rona and produced a daughter, Ros, who truly set the seal on his new life. Maybe there was something in grace after all. Certainly, most Americans he met socially or in the course of business felt entitled to a good life. He had not quite reached that stage of easy presumption and from time to time found himself waiting for the second shoe to fall. A worry wart, Rona called him whenever he doubted the permanence of success.

What did these workmen hope for, he wondered, as they toiled in the furnace heat, the sweat rolling down their faces under the hard hats? Most of them were black and came from DC. Not one of them lived in McLean which, apart from a few African diplomats, was a hundred percent white. It was well known in the trade that realtors, fearing a domino effect on house prices, refused to show any properties in McLean – or Bethesda or Chevy Chase – to a black family, however successful. The realtors would never admit to it of course, in case they aroused the ire of social justice warriors and other liberal groups.

What did these workmen hope for as they grafted in the blistering heat? Although the free market was supposedly a good thing he sometimes wondered if it couldn't be made a little more human. He and Rona were probably on one of the lower rungs of the one percent and it made him feel uneasy.

As the foreman shouted instructions to the crane driver, Niall checked the units on the flatbed truck against the invoice on his clipboard. He felt ineffectual, doing the minimum. The hard hats probably regarded him as a wimp. Yet he was glad to be out of the office.

"Are we on course for the deadline?" he asked.

The foreman shrugged. "I've had better crews. And the heat is murder. But with any luck we'll make it."

"I'll see if I can wrestle a bonus out of old Laughlin." Niall felt he could probably deliver on that. He was buoyed up by Ros's recent success and the way she – and Rona – took it in their stride as if they both had some cast-iron indemnity against failure.

He did some more paperwork in the site office, intrigued by the way some problems just disappeared of their own accord. There was something to be said for hastening slowly. He was learning all the time. By mid-morning he was back at headquarters, a nondescript building in DC with a McDonalds on one side and a Pizza Hut on the other. A map of the District hung behind his desk. This was his patch and he knew its anatomy down to the last infill site. His hi-tech briefcase lay open on the desk. It reminded him of an assassin's case, moulded inside for snug-fitting gun parts. This black fibre-glass model contained a tablet, a niche for assorted pens and a set of dividers for slim files. He carried his cell phone in the top pocket of whatever jacket he happened to be wearing; unlike most people he detested the phone and saw it as a necessary evil. He was in thrall to the damn thing but wanted to be rid of it and its incessant ringtone.

"Everything's OK on the site," he told Laughlin when he poked his long inquisitive head around the door. "How they can work so hard in this heat beats me."

"Hmmm," Laughlin muttered, as if his junior partner might not be the best of judges. Niall often felt that Laughlin did not rate him very highly, not that it bothered him much. His family was much more important to him than the job. Maybe he played second fiddle at home too, but that didn't bother him either; he was proud of the accomplishments of the two women in his life and had no difficulty basking in the glory they reflected on him.

At one o'clock he met Rona for lunch. They tried to meet once a week if at all possible; it was a pleasant little ritual they'd adopted when he turned forty. It was almost as sacrosanct as their Sunday morning four-ball at the country club. Today they chose *The Pigalle*, half-way along 18th Street – a slightly contrived French restaurant, Art Deco-ish but not too pretentious. The hostess seated them with a familiar smile.

"The Fall range arrived today," Rona said. She was a buyer for Bloomingdales and was enthusiastic about her job. She was dressed in a smart linen suit mercifully free of those Sumo shoulder pads that were in vogue years ago. Her smooth-skinned face dimpled with a smile. "Earth tones are back, thank god, and good fabrics. I think they'll sell well."

"I wouldn't doubt it," Niall said, referring to Rona's judgement rather than the fabrics. He glanced at the menu. "Six bucks for the prawns."

"Skinflint. Share the wealth."

"I'm not cheap, just frugal," he said with a grin. It was a variant of an old joke about insecurity. His. Maybe there was something in it. The need to put something by for an uncertain future, a lay-away plan. He wasn't a survivalist but he fully understood what motivated them. He hated credit cards; they were too slippery, untrustworthy. His grandmother used to sustain him with the sayings of Poor Richard on the virtues of thrift. He didn't realise until years later that Poor Richard was a character created by Benjamin Franklin. What goes around comes around. Like him, Rona had come up the hard way, working her way through college, but she never worried about finances or even about the future. Different mother's milk. Her confidence sometimes unnerved him but more and more it was beginning to rub off on him. Maybe positivity was a good thing, and didn't tempt fate.

"You know, if Ros flees the nest we'll be rattling around in the house on our own…" Rona paused over her starter. "Do you think we should move into an apartment?"

He felt uneasy. Decisions, rites of passage didn't appeal to him. The mere fact that Rona had mentioned the possibility of change made his heart skip a beat because she was obviously planning something. And her plans had a habit of being put into effect.

"We'll see," she relented. "It may not come

to that."

"You'd miss the garden," he pointed out. "All the work you've put in over the years." He shook his head at the magnitude of it all, the sacrifice.

"More time for golf though." She laid her fork aside and signalled to the waiter that they were ready for the main course.

"Golf, bridge and of course the Neighbourhood Watch," he murmured as if he were debunking the comfortable rut in which he wallowed.

"You should go for the firm," Rona said, sensing an opportunity.

"A lot of responsibility … too long in the tooth." Veins in his temples rippled as he chewed the veal. It was rather underdone but he didn't want to mention it since Rona would complain on his behalf. The course of least resistance suited him best; he chewed on manfully.

"Bullshit. You've more ability in your little finger than Laughlin has in his entire scrawny frame." Her fork hit the plate with a clatter, sending some seeds of rice onto the table cloth.

"More, more. I like it…"

"Be serious. You should be more positive. Don't give me that crap about being under the yoke of the invaders for seven hundred years. It's not in your goddam genes."

"Positive ions," he mused. "But positive genes? I wonder." He caught a glimpse of his face in an Art Nouveau mirror – a pale isosceles triangle like a parsnip tapering down to a narrow chin, the wire specs, a soft wart in the flange of his nose, the dark enervated tooth that Rona wanted him to have fixed. Not worth it in his estimation. It would take more than one sparkling canine to improve that mug. What had she ever seen in him?

"I'm not being the pushy American wife. And it's not about money. I just think you'd be more fulfilled if you took over the reins. You know the work inside out. You get on with the office staff and the building crews. There's no excuse for not using your potential. It's just such a waste."

"I'll think about it."

"Promise?"

"Promise." She really did believe in him. Was that part of his problem – that he mightn't be able to live up to her expectations? He had once toyed with the idea of therapy not so much because he felt neurotic but rather because he thought it might acculturate him to this strange, unrepentantly upbeat country of his adoption. But he couldn't do it. Mindfulness, encounter groups, schema therapy, all sounded so precious somehow. Also he had heard some bizarre stories – one involving a paedophile who was hugged by his group members in an effort to make him forgive himself, as if the perversion itself was of no significance. Besides, Niall didn't know how to bleed on the carpet. Instead, he tried, not very successfully, to follow Rona's example of natural, free and easy emotional honesty. Ros, of course, had the same gift.

"Ros has this party on Saturday night."

"She told me about the arrangements," Rona said. "Sounds like it's going to be a blast … I mean," she translated for him, "very enjoyable."

Niall wondered what that actually meant – enjoying a party. Eat, drink, dance, all three – so what? You could do all of that at home. Somehow he couldn't see Ros dancing on table tops, although it was quite conceivable that she did. He suspected that her mother had done her fair share of that sort of thing before they'd met. He had seen her kick up her heels at Captain's Prize night at the golf club on a couple of occasions when his own embarrassment was tempered by envy of her extroversion.

"She deserves to have a good time." Recollections scrolled through his mind – birthday parties at Virginia Beach with David and Mark, listening to the kids discuss the latest video games, trips to the Tidal Basin to see the cherry blossom in bloom, Easter-egg rolling on the White House lawn, visits to the Smithsonian to see spaceships and dinosaur skeletons. He was so relieved she'd had a normal childhood. And it was all suitably crowned by the recent conferring ceremony in Georgetown, which probably meant more to Niall than to Ros. He sat in the Great Hall with Rona watching everything, especially Ros in her gown and mortar board, smiling brilliantly as she received her scroll. He was amazed at her poise as she sailed through the ceremony. He, by contrast, was overcome by the occasion. At one point, after the presentation, he had Ros pose with her mother for a photograph. When he saw them framed in the viewfinder, these two women who were more than a part of his life, he almost lost control of his tear ducts. After that he had to force himself to play it cool so as not to embarrass Ros as she introduced him and Rona to her friends and their parents. It had been some topping-out ceremony, never to be forgotten.

"I'm paying today," he said when the bill arrived.

"It's not your turn," Rona objected. "What's gotten into you?"

"Just natural generosity of spirit." He riffled through his wallet for good old-fashioned paper money. She went to the ladies and he watched her walk every step of the way. They would probably have had more children except that she had miscarried a Down's syndrome baby and they were scared to try again. The fear was more on his side; typically he didn't want to push his luck. Rona once said to him, "For an erstwhile religious man you sure don't trust your Maker all that much." She had a point. His god, though not quite punishing, was tough and sometimes unfair, a stern superior keeping his subordinates on their toes. So, Ros became the single nucleus of the family.

They separated in the carpark, waving to

each other as they drove towards different exists.

That afternoon he met some clients interested in the new Potomac Development. He went over the drawings with them and meticulously noted their individual requirements, promising to get back to them with costings. He also had a meeting with Laughlin about the firm's own quarterly accounts. It was shaping up to be another good year.

At around five-thirty he drove over to Embassy Row to collect David, who was part of the car pool. David didn't keep him waiting; he was already on the pavement.

"Hop in, you old clock-watcher," Niall greeted him. "Anything stirring in the geo-political sphere today?"

"Nothing a few martinis can't solve," David said. "Why've you got the top up?"

"The air-conditioning works better." Niall had paid a lot for the option of a soft top only to find that it was no use in the summer months.

"And it's going to get hotter," David said, sitting into the front seat of the Chevrolet Malibu. Awful thought."

They waited until Si Wrexham, the third member of the car pool, showed. He owned and managed a catering company that specialised in Embassy receptions. In less than a minute he appeared around the corner, walking slowly to avoid a sweat, and hopped into the back of the car.

"Chocks away," Si said, "Truck at your six

o'clock."

Niall waited for a break in the traffic and then moved off from the kerb. Because he now had two passengers he was able to use the less congested High Occupancy Freeway. He fairly zipped along through the shimmering heat haze that rose from the asphalt.

"Any sign of you Brits throwing a bash soon?" Si inquired of David, who was extinguishing his first cigarette and blowing smoke from the side of his mouth towards the open window.

"As a matter of fact I think the ambassador is planning something fairly big in a couple of weeks at his residence…"

"A marquee job?" Si asked.

"I suppose so."

"We'll definitely tender for that. A kind word wouldn't hurt."

"A kind word never hurts." David said. He was looking forward to putting his feet up, reading the latest Lee Child with a pitcher of martinis at his side. In anticipation he lit another cigarette, bringing him up to the maximum the car pool allowed him. The rules were still evolving, however, and it was likely that they would soon ban smoking completely. They were going to have to clean up their act where the Neighbourhood Watch was concerned as well. Some months ago when they were patrolling their patch at night in David's jeep, Si had brought along a bottle of Canadian sipping whiskey, ostensibly to keep the cold out. When, in the early hours of the morning, they made their report to the police in Balls' Hill Road, they were politely but firmly told to go home and sleep it off. Si was also relieved of the baseball bat which he insisted on bringing along.

"There was something in the diplomatic bag today about Brexit and the hi-tech border between Southern and Northern Ireland," David said. "Whitehall thinks the damned IRA might start mobilising again. It defies logic, after all the effort that was put into the peace process."

"There's fault on all sides." Niall didn't want to get dragged into an argument but he couldn't avoid the suspicion that David was goading him. He concentrated on driving as he deftly changed into the inside lane of the George Washington Parkway. It occurred to him how little he knew about the IRA or what motivated them. His old school pal, Gerry, who lived in Dublin, sometimes phoned or emailed him with snippets of information but Niall had some doubts about the objectivity of the opinions expressed.

"You don't take a great interest in the old country," Si said to him.

"I'm a bit out of touch," Niall conceded. It was true; he didn't make any great effort to keep up. In a way he was glad to be free of the historical baggage and the ambivalent feelings one had for the underdog, however violent. America was fresh, uninhibited, and had the vigour of youth. The recent wars in Iraq and

Afghanistan, he hoped were exceptions that proved the rule.

"Ireland should be re-united anyway," Si remarked. "Hey, watch your three o'clock."

"It is a very complex issue…" David began.

"That's a crock," Si interrupted. "You bureaucrats make everything more complicated than it is. Gives you more paper to shuffle around. If it was a problem between two companies in the private sector it'd be solved in a week. The principals would be working on it around the clock."

"Especially if you were providing the canapés," Niall said, hunched up over the steering wheel as if afraid it might develop a mind of its own.

"Maybe there's something in that," David conceded. "We tend to be a bit cautious in the public sector. And no one wants to take an initiative in case it backfires politically."

"Yeah, well if we don't take initiatives in our work it hits the bottom line. Right Niall?" Si leant forward from the back seat to make his point more forcibly.

"I don't know," Niall said. "I think anyone can make a living in the property business. You don't have to be a dynamo. It's not all that risky." He certainly didn't regard himself as a risk-taker, and he had survived the bloodbath of 2008 reasonably well. Rona was on the hazard more than he was. All he had to do was put in the hours, liaise with the builders and architects and provide an efficient service for clients. The property values just went up and up as Washington became the political cockpit of the known world. What really amazed Niall though was that no one begrudged him his success – or at least he didn't think so. He was in the right place at the right time; good luck to him. The attitude seemed to be: if it happened to you maybe it can happen to me some day.

He dropped Si off first and watched him give the lawn sprinkler a wide berth as he walked up the short driveway and kicked a basketball out of his way.

"His lawn is badly burnt up," Niall remarked. "He left the sprinkling too late if you ask me."

David made no response; tending lawns wasn't high on his list of priorities – if indeed he had such a list. Niall put the car in gear and headed for Old Kirby Road. Just before he dropped David off he said, "Don't forget, dinner tomorrow at our place."

"No, but I hope Rona won't try and fix me up again." David gave him a sidelong glance.

"I'm innocent of any ulterior motive," Niall said with a grin. He and Rona knew of his 'nooner' arrangement and Rona, in particular, wanted to get him into a 'proper relationship'. "I think she just wants to make sure you have a square meal every now and again."

"Well, I appreciate that… By the way, I meant to ask you how the conferring went?"

"Oh, fine," Niall said. He didn't want to

elaborate since Mark hadn't made it.

"Mark is such a problem now," David volunteered. "My fault, I suppose, dragging him around the globe…"

"Don't blame yourself. It's your job. He'll straighten himself out in time. You'll see. Some kids mature faster than others."

"Touch wood," David said and then became more reflective. "I don't understand it though… My old man used to say, 'Put 'em before the mast.' And he did too. I had my Master's Ticket and had seen half the world before I was twenty-two. And before that I spent twelve years in a tough boarding school…" He shrugged. "Things are different nowadays, I suppose … snowflakes and all that. Well, thanks for the lift, old man." He got out of the car.

Niall drove on to his own house which was just a few hundred yards further along the same stretch of road. Yes, his lawn was in much better heart. And the house, which initially he had doubts about mainly because of the pretentious pillars modelled on the White House, had eventually won him over. As had the maintenance-free plastic siding – although the timber-frame construction sometimes gave him pause for thought and he was most diligent about calling in the Orkin men every year or so to check for termites. It was a large, colonial-style house, impressive by any standards, but the absence of concrete blocks or bricks sometimes made him wonder if it wasn't part of the set of

'Gone with the Wind'. Substance was the issue.

He went through the split-level lounge into the kitchen and started on the evening meal. He emptied the dishwasher, set the table and put the surplus crockery away. He set a place for Ros in case she wanted to eat before going out to her party. He checked on the pasta; it was coming along nicely. He added a little salt and nutmeg and snorted the warm odours that burst out of the saucepan.

When Rona got home he had a Campari and soda waiting for her. She kicked off her shoes and sat down with her drink.

"That's three you owe me," he reminded her.

"Who's counting?"

"I am."

"You know you like spoiling me. You're a New Ager aren't you? And you sprang for lunch today. What's going on? You must be having an affair." She grinned at him over the rim of her glass. He liked her in this kittenish mood.

"Yeah," he said, peering again into the saucepan, "I'm joining David in his nooners. We've made a foursome." He put down the ladle and sat on the arm of her chair, cradling her head against his side. He remembered that moment when he caught her and Ros in the viewfinder of the camera. They were laughing and, like a fool, he was on the verge of tears. "It's not a bad life, is it, Rona?"

"Not too bad, lover." She reached up and stroked the side of his face. When she finished her drink she went upstairs to change into more comfortable clothes. Attracted by the smell of food Hamm, the spaniel, started to snuffle around the kitchen. Niall spooned chunks of doggie food into his dish which narrowed at the rim to prevent the long ears from flopping into the comestibles.

Ros entered in a flurry, gave her father a peck on the cheek, and ran upstairs to shower and change her clothes. Niall listened to the muffled sounds of ablutions and chat from upstairs; to his ears it was lyrical.

Eventually they came down and joined him in the lounge. Rona was in jeans and Ros had her party gear on.

"Have you time for dinner here with us?" Niall asked.

"Sorry, Dad. No time. I have to be in Georgetown by seven-thirty. A few of us have booked a table in the 'Gattopardo'." She patted Hamm's head, looked at her watch and told them she'd probably sleep over in Gillian's house. Her parents wished her well.

"Take care," Niall added as Ros skipped down the steps towards her car. The screen door slammed after her. It would never be opened by her again.

CHAPTER 3

AFTER SEVERAL MARTINIS it took David a while to wrestle himself out of the recliner and fumble his way up to his bedroom. He continued reading in bed, dozed for a while, the open book lying face down on his chest. At about three in the morning he was awakened by a squeal of brakes and the sound of garbage cans being knocked over. Mark! Christ, what now?

He threw on a robe and rushed downstairs to see Mark stagger out of the jeep and move unsteadily towards the front door. He helped him into the house.

"What the hell have you been up to?" It hadn't escaped his notice that the front of the jeep was smashed in.

"Stuck up … bitch … her own fault." Mark fell against a side table, knocking it over.

David's blood ran cold. "Who … who?" While be manhandled his son towards the downstairs bathroom he asked more questions and gradually pieced together the fragments. When he knew there was no room for doubt, bile came to his throat and he vomited into the toilet. He stripped Mark and pushed him into the shower where he slumped against a tiled wall.

He left him there and searched Mark's room and the jeep for a burner phone, without success. He rang the Crime Stoppers number, giving a false name, saying he had witnessed a car going off the GW Parkway into the Potomac. It was an accident. He refused to be drawn on details and hung up. There was nothing more he could do. Except get Mark away somewhere. To alibi him. He owed him that much. Mark was still out cold. He left him in the shower, not knowing how long it would take to get him sobered up.

David prowled around the house, his mind in turmoil. Eventually, though he knew it was a desperation measure, he got into the jeep and drove back down the Parkway. Was it possible that Mark had just been hallucinating? For the first time in his life he prayed to some spiritual power to undo the nightmare. But then he saw the sirens of the police cars and rescue vehicles. Under powerful lights a huge crane was being driven into position on the roadway, its jib already stretching out over the Potomac. He even glimpsed the broken wall above the river before he took the off ramp and doubled back. Sweat ran down his forehead and into his eyes, blurring his vision. Unable to trust his reflexes, he eased back on the accelerator. As he passed the Grenham's house, he noticed that all the lights were out. He imagined Rona and Niall sleeping peacefully, unaware of what had happened. When would they get the call, hear the knock on the door?

Mark was still semi-comatose in the shower, mumbling incoherently. David shook him roughly but to no avail. He looked at the crumpled form with the same loathing he felt for himself. He went outside, kicked off his shoes and dived into the pool. Blood pounded in his ears as he swam a length under water; then he surfaced gasping for air. His rhythm was off but he fought his way up and down the pool, reversing in his own wash, giving his heart something to hammer against. The cicadas, silenced by the initial splash, began their mating calls again. David swam up and down ceaselessly, the cold water of the pool eliminating the sweat even as it formed on his body. He was overdoing it but he couldn't stop. He wanted to exhaust himself, to feel physical pain as if that might somehow obliterate the awful knowledge that lodged in his head.

At about 4.30 in the morning Mark had recovered just enough to be mobile. David helped him dress and plied him with black coffee. He drove him to Reagan Airport. They spoke little and then only in brief exchanges about where Mark should stay and how much money he would need. As they drove by the Tidal Basin with the early light bathing the cherry blossom, the events of the previous night seemed to melt away. Was it possible that Mark had forgotten them? Blackouts were the saving grace – or the deadly trap – of addicts, sparing them from the terrifying effects of the madness. On the other hand, Mark did not ask any questions about where or why he was being sent away. He knew; he knew all right.

David waited until he boarded the Eastern

shuttle. Mark went straight through the gate without once looking back; his head was bowed as if he were the victim.

The morning had matured when David got back to his house. This Saturday was going to be a scorcher. During the short walk from the air-conditioned jeep to his front door sweat seeped through his shirt which clung to his back like a poultice. From his front porch he looked towards the Grenham house. The curtains were pulled open which meant that Rona and Niall were up, and the two cars in the double garage suggested they were indoors. It seemed unlikely they had got the news yet.

Just then he saw Niall emerge and gesture to him. David's heart lurched. He hadn't put the jeep in the garage but at least the damaged fender was facing the house. Niall walked towards him, his face grave. What did it portend? With an effort of will David left his own porch to meet him half way – under a magnolia tree that was bursting with blossom.

"You're out and about early," David said.

"We'd planned to see the exhibition of Russian icons in the Smithsonian before it gets too crowded…"

"Well worth a visit, I hear," David said. He looked at his feet which were half covered in fallen magnolia petals.

"By the way, did you or Mark happen to see Ros?" Niall rubbed his unshaven face.

"No." The inevitability of the question made

David sick to his stomach. Instinctively he moved deeper into the shade of the tree, but absolute blackness would have been preferable. He placed a hand on the tree trunk to steady himself.

"She stayed at Gillian's but it's unlike her not to phone…" Niall glanced at his watch which caught a flare of sunlight. " … by this time … Any sign of Mark? I presume he was at the party too."

"No…" David began.

"Oh, right," Niall said in some embarrassment. Since Mark hadn't made the cut it was unlikely that he'd have turned up at the celebration.

"He's in New York, as a matter of fact."

This didn't seem to register with Niall who said, "Well, if you see her…" He trailed off.

"Of course." David wanted to add something like, "She'll turn up; you know what kids are like." But he couldn't bring himself to say that. "Of course," he repeated. "Sure."

"I'd better get back to Rona." Niall re-crossed the street. David noticed he was wearing carpet slippers.

About an hour later Rona and Niall could wait no longer. She put through a call to Gillian who said she was surprised that Ros had not turned up at her place the night before.

"I assumed she went … straight home from the party," Gillian added uncertainly, afraid of saying the wrong thing.

Rona pressed her for more details in an effort to discover a rational explanation, other possibilities. Gillian had nothing more to offer. Rona placed her cell phone on the table and turned to face Niall who stood behind her as if in a trance. They stared at each other for a long time, seeking reassurance in each other's eyes.

When David got back to his own house he leant against the door which closed behind him; he began to shake. When after a couple of drinks, he felt reasonably composed, he drove to Tyson's Corner where he left the jeep to be repaired in an unfamiliar garage. He paid the emergency charge up front and then went to a cinema where he dozed fitfully. He sat through the film a second time, welcoming the dark and the isolation and the flickering images that sometimes caught his attention and distracted him for a time. He thought of calling Julie but Saturday was her day off. In any case he was afraid he might come unglued with her and cause her to suspect something. There was only one way to handle the situation; the hard way. And it was going to get harder.

When he got home he started to drink with a vengeance, throwing the stuff back as if he hated it. From the front bay window he could see a corner of Niall's house; it looked no different.

Had they not heard yet? When would they get the call that would mark them forever, the news that they would reject at first until the words, repeated over and over, would finally be driven in like rivets?

Sprawled on a sofa in the darkening room, he became maudlin in drink. "…not my fault…" he thought. "Jesus, why am I involved in this? That pup's dropped me in it … left me to pick up the pieces." He held up his hands, palms to the front as if he were trying to push away this awful responsibility that had descended unfairly on him. Just before he passed out he thought he saw a car pull up across the street.

That was the recollection that drummed through his brain when he came to on Sunday morning. He could lie low for the day, not answering phone or door; that indeed was his preference. But what about Monday? Niall would not turn up for the car pool and he would have to make inquiries then. Better to confront now, he thought, a pre-emptive strike would strengthen the alibi, reinforce innocence. They would be in a state of shock anyway and wouldn't be able to see through his performance.

He was just about to have a hair of the dog to strengthen his resolve when the doorbell rang. He peered out the window first. Si .What the hell did *he* want? He opened the door and let him in.

"Hi Dave … My god you must've had a hard night. You look wrecked." Si himself was a contrast-gainer; he looked disgustingly fit and energetic.

"What's up?" David looked warily at him.

"You've forgotten, haven't you?"

"What?" David asked irritably. He was at a disadvantage in more ways than one and didn't appreciate Si's taunting questions at this hour of the morning.

"We're taking a bunch of Webelows on a hike around Bull Run. Departing the fix at nine hundred. They're waiting at my place. Come on, get the lead out."

David passed a hand across his aching forehead. He remembered now, but the thought of leading a group of scouts on a twelve-mile hike terrified him. "I can't…"

"What do you mean, 'can't'? Sure you can. Fresh air is what you need." He expanded and slapped his ample chest by way of illustration.

"No, I mean I'm on standby … The embassy…" He knew it was lame but he was daunted by Si's take-charge manner and yen for the great outdoors.

"Oh yeah, like you're James Bond or something. The Cold War is over, haven't you heard? And Britannia doesn't rule the waves anymore. C'mon, kick the tyres and light the fires." Si grinned hugely. He'd started his catering career in the Air Force and liked to use the heroic patois of the fliers and top guns even though he himself had never been inside a cockpit in his life.

"Really," David said with as much gravitas

as he could muster. "I'm stuck here. We have a senior political figure arriving this afternoon … I did forget the hike and I'm sorry. I'll make it up to the scouts another time." He hoped that would do it; his resistance was flagging and he began to feel faint.

"We-e-ell, OK," Si conceded. "But we need your jeep."

David fetched the keys from the mantelpiece and threw them to him. Si caught them with a flourish.

"Don't sacrifice your liver for your country," Si advised. He had catered enough embassy functions to know how much hard liquor diplomats could put away. They called it work. He jiggled the keys in his hand. "Tailwinds," he said as he left, closing the door after him.

David poured himself a large measure of neat vodka and brought it with him into the bathroom where he spruced himself up as best he could. He changed his clothes and cleaned his teeth a second time, hoping the toothpaste would disguise his liquor breath. He summoned all his courage and walked to the front door of the Grenham house. With every step he felt his skull lift, but he had to go through with it. The door was opened by the local doctor who told him what had happened. David stood in front of him, unable to react or say anything.

"You can't do anything now, David," Dr. Murray said. "They're under sedation. I'll tell them you called."

"I … I…"

"I can see you're in shock. Go home and pour yourself a stiff drink."

David nodded. Having psyched himself up for the moment of confrontation, he now had a short-lived sense of relief as he went back to the prison of his empty house.

Rona felt as if she were being pulled downwards into deep water. She struggled for a while but then realised that she didn't really want to swim towards the light or break the surface. Something bad was waiting for her, something monstrous but her memory could not articulate it. She heard the slow rhythm of Niall's drugged sleep; it lulled her back to a preferred state of unconsciousness.

Later that night Niall got up quietly and went downstairs in his bare feet as if he were sleepwalking. He was searching for something but didn't know what. Habit led him towards the fridge which he stared at for a while before turning away in confusion. He padded silently into the sitting room and stood looking at the door that had closed behind Ros the last time he saw her. But he wasn't able to make that connection and didn't know why he was drawn towards the door. Nevertheless he continued to stare at it, vaguely conscious of the purring of the air-conditioning system. Eventually he went back to the bedroom, still wondering why he had gone downstairs. Unable to remember, he slipped back into bed – quietly so as not to wake his wife. Because of her job she had an earlier start in the morning than he did. She needed her sleep.

After an autopsy and forensic examination the body was released for burial by the County Coroner. Some alcohol had been found in the blood stream and a verdict of accidental death was returned. A precinct captain rang one of his friends in the Roads Department to tell him that the camber of the road at the site of the accident was deficient in his view, and that the wall should be replaced by crash barriers. His contact in the Roads Department said they would fix it, but not immediately in case it sparked off litigation.

Rona and Niall were brought by a patrolman to the county morgue to identify the body of their daughter. Like soldiers who had sustained massive wounds they were mercifully numb and cold as ice; the pain would come later. When the sheet was pulled back, Rona kissed her daughter's face and smoothed a strand of hair back from the pale forehead. Niall stared and stared, uncomprehending.

"This is your daughter, Ros Grenham?" The

coroner's voice reverberated in the vaulted space.

"Of course," Niall said. He signed a form that was put in front of him then reached out to Rona who was beginning to crumple.

Her brother, a doctor from Milwaukee, made most of the arrangements though he tried to involve Rona and Niall in them as much as possible, on the grounds that any activity – even choosing a casket – could be therapeutic. He talked to them about the grieving process and the importance of 'closure'. The loss of a child, he told them, was the most traumatising because it went against the natural order of things. Up to the day of the funeral the house was full of friends and relatives, some of them sleeping over. Rona's parents were prepared to stay indefinitely; they were shattered by the death of their only granddaughter. Rona seemed to appreciate the company and the activity, being crowded with kindness. Niall was moved by it too but he found it hard to concentrate and tended to drift in and out of reality. Once, when he was exhausted, he dozed for a while in a chair and a picture of the crucifixion entered his head. The dying Christ looked down at him; the hooded eyes opened slowly and the compassionate expression changed gradually to one of amusement. "What did you expect?" The words were spoken by a voice that sounded familiar.

David left nothing to chance and made sure

Mark returned for the funeral. They stood at the edge of the group in the cemetery under the shade of a stand of cypress trees. A blanket of vivid green Astro turf covered the spoil from the open grave while some distance away a mechanical excavator waited, its driver leaning against a giant wheel, smoking a cigarette. Mark kept shifting his feet and scratching his arms. He was probably in withdrawal, more concerned about his next fix than the burial of his childhood friend and victim.

"For god's sake, stop fidgeting," David said in a stern whisper. On the other side of the grave he saw Rona leaning against Niall, their arms around each other. Spectral in the heat haze, their faces were a ghastly white against their black clothes, clowns' faces almost.

After the ceremony David shook Niall's hand and embraced Rona. "If there's anything … anything…"

"I know." Rona nodded in appreciation.

Mark followed suit. "I'm … so sorry, Mr. and Mrs. Grenham…"

"It's hard on you too, Mark," Rona said. "You were … contemporaries … friends."

David sat hunched in the jeep. The responsibility for inflicting such pain was unbearable. He watched Mark get into the passenger seat; his eyes slid off him. He drove quickly away from the cemetery.

Later, over a barely touched casserole left by his part-time housekeeper, Mark raised his head to say, "It wasn't my fault." In the ensuing silence he ran the tips of his fingers across his forehead; he touched his face frequently. David wondered if it wasn't some kind of nervous tic. He wanted to ignore the protestation of innocence but could not restrain himself.

"An accident, was it?"

"Yes, an accident."

"How did it happen?"

"A skid…"

"In this dry weather? In a four-wheel drive vehicle?" David pushed the plate away from him; his stomach churned with shame and barely concealed anger.

"Look, if you don't believe…"

"It's not a question of belief. It's knowledge. *I know* you were completely out of it that night. Was it an accident that you took those drugs? Did someone tie you up and force them down your throat or into your veins? Did they put you in the jeep and start it up…?"

"Believe what you like. You never listened to me anyway. Why start now?"

"What I don't know is … whether it was … deliberate." David said the last word under his breath; he was afraid of it.

"For Christ's sake! You never believed anything I…" He got up abruptly and left the room. David's first instinct was to follow and knock sense into him, make him take responsibility for what he had done. But he knew it would be futile, just as the one and only therapy session had been futile. It had taken eighteen months of nonstop badgering to get Mark into a treatment programme. The counsellor, an earnest young woman, had explained how many addicts needed highs as a substitute for parental affection. Any altered state was preferable to reality and they came to depend on those blissed-out feelings. When sober, they screened out the junk sickness, remembering only the highs. Euphoric recall was very powerful. Mark, she opined, wanted to keep up with the smart set but couldn't, mainly because of a poor self-image. So he went to the other extreme. David listened in silence. This was the greatest drivel and liberal psychobabble he'd ever heard. No wonder drug-taking had reached epidemic proportions. He had known several dipsos in the Navy. A good skipper could scare them straight and usually did. The choice was simple: no grog on deck or no grog in the brig. The modern approach was a waste of time and indeed it had no influence whatsoever on Mark, who simply walked out of the clinic one morning and was meeting his dealer on 14th Street that very afternoon.

After that they more or less divided the house between them and went their separate ways. No doubt Mark missed his mother but what could David do about that? Introduce him to Julie, his pay-as-you-go lover? It was a godawful mess and it was foolish to think in terms of a solution. It was up to Mark to determine his own future, if he had one.

So when he announced that he was going back to New York, David didn't try to stand in his way; in fact he was relieved – for both their sakes.

CHAPTER 4

THE TRUST FUND his mother had set up for him, some years before her death, was dwindling fast but Mark still had about four thousand dollars left. When that ran out he could probably count on the old man who had always been less tight with money than he was with time. It was possible that the accident had changed all that but Mark really didn't think so. Blood was thicker than water, and all that shit. Besides, his opinionated Dad was not willingly going to let his son be handed over to the American justice system which he regarded as a joke.

For the first week or so Mark stayed in a cheap hotel just off Times Square where he had already made the necessary contacts. He had to stay reasonably clean until he found his feet. The events of that unfortunate night, insofar as he could remember them, did unsettle him and he found that a combination of methadone and bourbon helped keep his head straight without spacing him out.

He had spent the first couple of days looking for a service-type job in the restaurants of Midtown which hired harpists and cellists from Juilliard, but he soon lowered his sights, crossed the class divide of Houston Street and was taken on as a bus boy and general factotum in a late-night Italian place on Mott Street. It paid eight dollars an hour, a share of the tips and all the leftover pasta he could eat. As he got to know the state of the kitchen he indulged rather sparingly in the latter. Oddly enough, the job gave him a sense of security even though the owner, Francesco Carli, bawled him out at every hand's turn. Mark didn't take it too seriously since, as far as he was concerned, that was just the way Italians carried on.

On the evening of his first day a part-time waitress, Sue, caught his attention. She wasn't particularly striking – indeed was a bit down-at-heel – but there was something about her that interested him, especially when he noticed her slipping into the restroom and emerging with a rather vacant smile on her face, a smile which she didn't attempt to conceal when she saw him looking at her. It didn't take long before they were pooling their resources and taking their hits together.

Eventually he moved into her room at the top of a semi-derelict building on Elizabeth Street close to the point where Little Italy blended into Chinatown. Although they slept together it was chemical dependency that bonded them. They rarely got up before noon; then they would watch daytime soaps sitting cross-legged on the fold-away bed – that was never folded away – with damp towels around their naked bodies, trying to keep cool right under the pitched ceiling that pressed down on them, especially where the eaves sagged under the weight of the water tower.

If the stash ran low Mark would go out into the street to replenish supplies. He would look for the regular dealer who worked the northeast section of the Bowery. Failing that, he would wait until a watermelon man approached him, materialising out of the fume-filled street. Once, Mark came back light.

"That's all…?" Sue queried. "A dime bag?" She ran a hand irritably through her lank hair, then rubbed it on her tee-shirt at waist level.

"Temporary shortage," Mark said though he had kept the coke for himself. He believed in having his own stash for emergencies; addicts were perfect capitalists. He had already done a line in a phone booth on the way back and was beginning to feel the effects.

Sue fetched a needle from a tin box under the bed and began searching for a vein, tapping her arm in a professional, medical way.

"We have to go to work later…" Mark cautioned.

"So?" She didn't look up from her labours which absorbed her completely.

"Just take it easy." But in a way he admired her. There were no limits where her habit was concerned. She was an oil-burner and that somehow reassured him; by comparison he was hardly addicted at all.

She gave him a withering look. "Hey, I've been managing on my own long before you showed up."

"Yeah?" He made a point of looking around

the crummy room which was something between a rat's nest and a bolt hole.

"Yeah." Her attention had now shifted to the inside of her left thigh which she probed and tapped with the minute curiosity of a child.

"Coping maybe, but managing … I think not."

"Don't fucking patronise me." She glared at him, noticing the way his lip curled on the barb. It was the way her father used to sneer before he laid into her with his fists. She had quit that scene when she was sixteen and if Mark ever tried that on he'd get more than he bargained for. There was only one remedy for violence; that was why she carried a fish-knife in her bag.

"I'm just pointing out some facts," he said. "Or rather one big economic fact."

"I could point one out to you. What about Ros?"

"What?"

"You heard me. A couple of nights ago you nodded out and started squawking about her … You've got a past you'd like to forget."

He wanted to know what exactly he'd said, but asking would be a kind of admission, definitely a sign of weakness. So he simply murmured in a conciliatory tone, "Haven't we all?" He thought there was a reasonable possibility she'd forget all about it after a few more scores. He'd be more generous with her the next time.

"Maybe." She was keen enough to make

peace too, at least for the moment. Although his clothes were far from pristine she could tell that they were of good quality – Bloomingdales at a guess – and she surmised that he had money, or at least access to it. And he had no qualms about tracking down dealers on the street; this proved to facilitate her habit. Still finding it hard to rope a vein, she decided to chase the dragon instead. She heated the H in a spoon over the gas jet and inhaled deeply. The rush was sudden and exhilarating, infusing her whole body. Overwhelmed by feelings of warmth, and heedless of consequence, she demanded sex which he, rather indifferently, agreed to, letting her ride him wildly, vaguely conscious of the slapping of their sweat-soaked bodies. Smacked out, she climaxed again and again while he, keyed to a different chemistry, wanted it to last a long time while his mind played out and savoured those major guitar chords which in reality he had never mastered.

Later that evening the restaurant was so busy and the clientele so loud that their mistakes simply got absorbed into the general chaotic swing of things. Even Francesco, who fawned over one particular all-male party, failed to notice that Sue got her table orders mixed up more than once. Mark covered for her a couple of times but for the most part he was almost invisible in the steamy kitchen, surrounded by sweating men in greyish undershirts. The ripe cheeses and rich sauces coalesced into a smell of puke.

His father should see him now, Mark thought, diplomat's son and heir, feeding swill to this boorish clientele. The family folklore included a ne'er-do-well uncle who had been sent as a remittance man to Australia. Mark too was a substandard export, keeping up the family tradition. While his old man had alibied him, that was to avoid scandal, a whiff of which would send shock waves through the diplomatic corps. As he dumped soiled tablecloths into a laundry hamper it occurred to him that he might have more leverage than he realised in extracting a considerable remittance in return for lying low. If he played his cards right he could be free of all constraints; it was a comforting thought.

Freedom was what he'd always wanted, the freedom to do whatever he liked and to be his own man. His father couldn't afford to let himself down in front of the Yankees whom the British had civilised in the first place, but who now ruled the roost. His father's obsession with appearances and proprieties would keep Mark free and safe; in a way it had already done so.

CHAPTER 5

RONA'S BROTHER PERSUADED her to go for bereavement counselling and although Niall went with her to the first few sessions his heart wasn't really in it. Pain, he believed, had to be endured; there were no circuit-breakers or feel-good reprieves. He found it difficult to understand how Rona could unburden herself to a total stranger, however sympathetic, and collapse into tears as she did on several occasions. It seemed as if she were putting herself through hell by deliberately re-living the events. Maybe she would recover more quickly because of that but for him recovery was not an option; it would never happen and could never happen for the simple reason that his beloved daughter was dead. He eventually cried off therapy and Rona continued to attend.

A curious thing happened about a fortnight after the funeral. He was taking the dog for a walk in a nearby wood where, years ago, he used to supervise Ros during her tree-climbing phase. He remembered how she would call down to him through the sunlit branches, giving an excited commentary on everything she discovered, especially birds' nests and the eggs which would later have to check out on the internet. He became disorientated and couldn't distinguish any of the landmarks he knew so well. It was as if a blanket of darkness had suddenly descended on him although it was still early evening. He panicked at first as the dark fog swirled around him, but then became strangely calm and sat motionless at the foot of a tree, as Hamm scampered about his outstretched legs. Some seven hours later Rona alerted the neighbours and it was Si who found him in the early hours of the morning. He was still seated in the same position, gently stroking the dog.

Shortly afterwards his immune system virtually shut down and he was afflicted by viral infections, including a rare form of shingles which left his face pockmarked above and below his left eye. During that period he was confined to bed. Rona took as much time off work as she could to look after him, bringing him chicken broth and beef tea which he often left untouched. He made several attempts to get on his feet, go back to work and take the pressure off Rona, but he simply didn't have the energy.

Old Laughlin retired in September and Niall did not enter the succession stakes. Nothing was further from his mind. The new senior partner called Rona to let Niall know that he was under no pressure to return to work and should take as much time as he needed to recuperate fully. On days like that Niall would come to the conclusion that people could be kind – unlike that spiritual Being to whom he once prayed and dedicated his life.

When he began to recover, following a series of massive injections of vitamin B – called

'Hollywood shots' by the GP – Rona delicately raised the question of their annual holiday. They had planned to go to Mexico for a couple of weeks, to explore the Mayan civilisation in the Yucatán Peninsula.

"I'd forgotten," Niall said. It was his second day out of bed and he was pruning roses in the garden. He laid the secateurs aside and rubbed a blister that had formed on his right hand. He had the impression that his hands had become thin and bony. They were a pen-pusher's hands of course that had never done any real work.

"It would be good for both of us," Rona said. Her brother had recommended it strongly, as had her group therapist.

"I … don't know…" Niall was a little taken aback. "I don't think … I'd be up to it." When they'd planned the trip Ros was to have accompanied them; it would probably have been their last holiday together as a family and it was Ros who had, since childhood, been fascinated by the Mayans. "Why don't you go …? You could bring Betty with you." Betty was Si's wife and would make an excellent travelling companion.

"I don't think so," Rona said. "It wouldn't be the same. Think about it. It would be a good way to recuperate. You need to build yourself up."

"I'll be fine. Anyway I'll have to go back to work soon." The low sun cast their shadows, long and parallel, on the grass. He went back to his pruning; she hadn't the heart to tell him it was the wrong time of year.

Closer to the house she passed a square patch of discoloured grass where the sand box used to be. She remembered Ros sitting there when she was five or six with what turned out to be a piece of crayon stuck up her nose. Having tried unsuccessfully to extract it with a tweezers, Rona hit on the bright idea of sprinkling pepper around, hoping she would sneeze it down. That didn't work either. Niall, who had begun to sneeze in sympathy, drove her with mounting panic to the nearest emergency department. When Ros saw a rather stern nurse approach her with an assortment of sinister looking tubes she began to cry and the tears washed down the crayon. On the drive home Ros sniffled in the back of the car mumbling, "…bad lady …bad lady," while Rona and Niall fought back the laughter of relief. Where was she now, their daughter?

The following morning as Rona drove into D.C. she passed the accident site. She had of course passed it several times since the tragedy but this time she forced herself to examine it. As the car slowed she noticed how the wall had been repaired. It looked strong and well-built. But was it any different to the original wall? She wasn't sure just then why the question entered her mind or what it might signify. Nausea filled her stomach and it took a while before she was able to drive on.

Niall worked in the garden for most of that

day. Grey-eyed, he gazed at the shrubs and trees beginning to shed, foliage and fruit rotting into the earth. The still unhealed pock marks on his face looked livid in the sunlight. It was ridiculous how absorbed he became in the tasks he set himself, but maybe that was one way of getting through bad times. Capsized lifeboats might eventually right themselves as long as they stayed above the surface. It was one of his rare positive thoughts and he resolved to help Rona more – as she had helped him through his illness. He knew that their lives would never be the same; they would have to accept that.

When he did go back to the office he received a warm welcome from the staff, most of whom had, as far as he could recall, attended the funeral. During the first few days individuals came into his office to offer condolences in private. They were ill at ease for the most part and it occurred to him how difficult it was for the citizens of a bounteous country to cope with death. But that made him appreciate their gesture all the more. The new owner, Jack Wyndham, offered to make him an equal partner if he increased his shareholding. Niall thanked him and said he'd think about it.

"Sure, Niall. Take your time. There's no hurry."

"I'd like to get my teeth into something," Niall said. There was nothing in his in-tray. He couldn't remember what he'd been working on before the accident but Jack, or old Laughlin, must have given it to someone else to complete.

"Of course … sure thing." Jack rang his secretary and asked her to get the file on a duplex development in Rosslyn. "I think the developer is a bit optimistic, Niall. Maybe if you could do an independent valuation … if you feel up…"

"Absolutely." Niall wondered if the project was completely necessary but, having been handed the file, he set to with a will.

It took the car pool a while to get back to normal. Si and David were a little reticent as if they needed permission to speak. When they did take the plunge their chat was desultory and rather strained. Si's shaggy dog stories were conspicuous by their absence, though he did remind them of the more light-hearted episodes in the car pool's history, such as the time when, for no apparent reason, they took on a hillbilly truck in a game of chicken along Dolly Madison Boulevard. Si was driving and the two vehicles sped along side by side for two miles, neither giving any quarter. Towards the end of the mad escapade David saw one of the hillbilly passengers reach behind him and pick up a pump action shotgun from the rack at the back of the cab. Si refused even then to abandon the race and only did so when his two passengers became almost hysterical. As he gradually fell back, swiping the steering wheel in frustration, a great rube "Yee-Haaaw" could be heard issuing from the truck that forged ahead in a cloud of exhaust fumes.

"We were younger then," David said.

"You were the one who needed the change of underwear," Si reminded him. He was glad to note that a faint smile had appeared on Niall's face.

"Those half-saved colonials can be quite intimidating," David conceded.

The problem was that normality could not be restored without effort, while the effort itself, in the circumstances, could never be subtle enough.

One evening as Niall was parking the car in his driveway he saw a smartly dressed black woman leaving the house. She gave him a nod and a half smile as she passed.

"Who was that?" he asked Rona when he got inside.

"Who?" She looked up from some paper work she was doing on the kitchen table. The autumn lines would be out soon and she had a lot of preliminary work to get through.

"That woman who was just here." He laid his briefcase aside and started to fill the kettle.

"A black woman?"

"Mmmm."

Rona hesitated before answering. "A private investigator…"

"What…?" He stood holding the kettle until it overflowed.

"A PI."

"A PI?" He tended to repeat things when he was confused or surprised. This sounded like something from a daytime soap; it was ludicrous. "Why on earth...?"

Rona gave a tough, barely perceptible, shrug and cut to the chase. "It may not have been an accident." She wasn't absolutely sure of herself and because of that the words came out more aggressively than she intended.

"...not have been an ... I don't follow." He sat down and faced her across the table. A chrome-and-glass pepper mill stood between them, a present from Ros on their fifteenth anniversary. She had always remembered birthdays too.

"A feeling ... call it a hunch," Rona said defensively.

It took him a while to absorb this. Had her action been prompted by her counsellor, he wondered; was it some form of sublimation? Had he wrongly assumed that the strength she had shown betokened a healing? There were different ways of trying to cope; he knew that. She went into Ros's room every day as if it were a shrine; he couldn't do that, not if his life depended on it.

"Rona, let it go." He placed his hand on hers and was surprised by how cold it felt. He massaged it gently for a while trying to get the blood going.

"I pass by that wall every day. And I remember what it was like before ... It was strongly built, Niall. A car going at 60 miles an hour wouldn't have crashed right through it... Besides, Ros was an excellent driver and she had good reflexes..."

"Yes, I know." Niall remembered that reflex-testing slot machine they used to have in Hechts in Tyson's Corner all those years ago. He used to let Ros beat him until the day came when he didn't have to pretend anymore. "But the police didn't suspect foul play," he pointed out. "And we had the Coroner's verdict of accidental death."

"The police haven't the resources. They're overstretched in this ... murder capital. According to Diane ... that woman ... they only concentrate on cases where firearms are involved. It's a question of priorities."

This was happening too fast for Niall. He feared that their daughter's death would be turned into some kind of melodrama. The very mention of private investigator and murder demeaned her memory. Who in god's name would have wanted her dead? It was crazy, obscene.

She mistook his silence for a rebuke. "I'm sorry. I should have mentioned it earlier."

"Are you sure you're doing this for ... the right reasons?"

"I've thought a lot about it." She didn't have to elaborate. Eventually he gave her the benefit of the doubt. Even though he couldn't see the point of her action he had always respected her judgement.

"How are you holding up?" He lit the gas under the kettle.

"Just keeping my head above water. You?"

"The same. Work helps a little bit."

"Yes."

"Will we ever…?"

"I don't think so." She shook her head slowly

"No." He put his arm around her shoulders. His wife. She had always thought life was fair whereas he had harboured doubts. Now they both knew.

David stopped seeing Julie. It hadn't exactly been a grand passion so the parting wasn't difficult and was in fact amicable enough. It bothered him a little that she would probably have a replacement for the Wednesday noon slot before the week was out. Still, the break was as clean and easy as he wanted it to be. That's what money bought: freedom from entanglements.

He now spent most of his two-hour lunch breaks in one or other of the museums and art galleries – the Corcoran was his favourite. It was a more edifying pastime on the whole and far less sweaty. He could spend ages looking at landscape paintings as long as they were conventional and representational.

His job at the embassy was much as before.

The Iraq war had in the past provided something of a buzz but it was over, and the ongoing conflict in Afghanistan was now much less newsworthy, so, he was now back to the old inane grind of financial reportage. He did what little he had to do, kept his head down and didn't socialise. The reports, drafted by his assistant and blue-pencilled by himself – usually to her chagrin – went off like clockwork in the pouch and, sometimes, by e-text on a secure line, the latter being quite unnecessary. There was a tendency to classify the most banal items as top-secret; it gave people a sense of importance. Also, old habits of paranoia died hard. David had once visited Budapest with an old MI5 spook in the seventies. Out of long habit, the agent did a sweep of the hotel room and to his horror discovered a whole network of wires under the carpet. Methodically, he cut them one by one – until a chandelier crashed to the ground in the room below. David dined out on the yarn for years though he never revealed the man's name.

He sometimes had a vision of his financial reports being received in Whitehall and going straight into the bin, or more likely, the shredder. Still, it was an easy job and a reasonably well paid one. He was also exempt from parking fines and state taxes on liquor, groceries and petrol. He was one of an army of expat Brits without an Empire to run; they were as inconsequential as grandfathers in a potting shed. Many CIA spooks had also become redundant following Glasnost, though they quickly reinvented themselves as the US grew its imperial tentacles. David knew some of those who lived near Langley; one of them had coached Mark in Little League. At least David could face the reality of a supernumerary life. There were others who couldn't, including the ambassador who adopted a florid didactic tone which grated on the nerves of his American counterparts who had more global fish to fry and who no longer regarded Britain as a major player. It was said of him that he'd once written to NBC asking them to take off the air a show that featured an English butler working for an *arriviste* American family.

Now that a couple of months had passed since the tragedy, David was almost ready to put the matter behind him. His damage limitation activities seemed to have worked. He regretted that the wedge between Mark and himself had been driven further in but there wasn't much he could do about that. Mark was old enough now to find his own feet if he had a mind to, and any further interference on David's part could only be counterproductive. A nervy kind of stability reigned, at least for a while.

On a still bright September evening as he carpooled home, Niall mentioned the fact that Rona had hired a private investigator.

"It can't hurt," was Si's verdict. "You never can tell." He was relieved that Niall now seemed prepared to talk things out. "No harm at all. None…"

"I suppose it's an understandable reaction," David said as neutrally as he could, trying to conceal the unease he felt.

"Apparently the police don't pay much attention nowadays unless guns are involved," Niall said. He wondered if he wasn't in a way seeking their approval. The idea of privatised justice was still foreign to him.

"Well, a PI would say that, I expect." David had a frightening intimation that it was all beginning again. He stroked his forehead and felt the damp on his fingertips.

"We've reached a sorry state in this country." Si shook his head. "A very sorry state." Turning to Niall he added, "If there's anything I can do…"

"That goes for me too," David said.

Later that night he called Mark, whose speech was slurred and virtually incoherent. David gave him the usual lecture on addiction but decided against telling him about the latest turn of events. It probably wouldn't have registered with him anyway.

CHAPTER 6

SOMETIMES NIALL THOUGHT the roads that cut through the suffocating greenery of Virginia seemed all wrong, out of time and place, and would sooner or later be reclaimed by the wilderness, by some inexorable law of nature. A few of the old theologians he had known in Maynooth believed passionately in the natural law as long as it was interpreted by "right reason," whatever that was. There were so many logical cop-outs, though he didn't recognise them as such at the time. The usual method of escaping from a logical impasse was by resorting to the notion of *mystery* which human minds by definition could not fathom.

There were many mysteries. His daughter's death was a mystery.

His mind began to race. What was he doing here, in this car, at this moment, on the way home from a particular job in a medium-sized city? What were his friends talking about – some item in the newspaper about the impeachment of a President, other scandals?

Vaguely he hears Si, "…that's nothing. You'd be amazed at the scams I've come across. A caterer is invisible to the guests, you see. They think he's a robot or part of the furniture. But he hears and sees everything. Yes sir, you'd be amazed. But it's like the seal of the confessional. You can't repeat anything you hear at these

functions. It would be wrong, unprofessional…"
He checked his rearview mirror and pumped the
brake pedal to warn off a U-Haul truck that had
come too close.

"Meaning you wouldn't get paid for it?"
David asked with a sardonic smile.

Niall sat in the back seat with head bowed,
hands resting on his knees.

"Wrong. You see people let their hair down
at these functions and the caterer must respect
that. Mind you, if you wanted to go in for
blackmail what better opportunity is there? Oh
yes, I've heard things at political gatherings
that'd make your hair curl. Governments have
fallen over less … Bastard!" Si swerved to let the
impatient U-Haul pass him on the inside.

"What sort of things?" David inquired
without much interest.

"Shortly after I started in this business we did
a CIA bash in the Hirshhorn Museum and I heard
this spook from Black Ops talking in his cups
about supplying a certain President with bugging
devices and truth drugs. The guy was boasting
about it. Loudly, I might add."

"And I suppose you heard something about
the JFK assassination?"

"Give us a break. I was only a toddler then."

"Too bad. You might have been able to
change the course of history."

"But another caterer who operated in the
Dallas area did get wind of it. It's well known in
the trade."

"I thought as much," David said in a weary tone that was only partially feigned. "Catering folklore is indeed a rich archive."

"Let's just say Oliver Stone's movie wasn't far off the mark. You think Washington's cleaned up its act since then? Uh-huh. It's worse than ever now." He looked back over his shoulder to see if Niall was paying attention. "I reckon that every politician makes his salary twice over in kickbacks from lobbyists. At least twice. And the military brass aren't exempt either. The Iraq war was a bonanza for the arms industry and those guys know who their friends are. Long before it became public knowledge we in the catering trade knew they were using depleted uranium in anti-tank shells. Nuclear weapons, for Christ's sake."

"Hindsight," David said.

"No sir. We knew in advance. And we also got advance notice of renditions and 9/11. But rightly or wrongly, our ethical code requires us to keep all such Intel to ourselves. If all the so-called intelligence agencies really wanted an effective way to gather information they should set up a catering firm. But don't repeat that. Who needs more competition..." He droned on, filling to the brim what otherwise might have been silences.

Niall was surprised to see Rona playing home movies and it was obvious that she'd been crying. She switched off the DVD player as soon as he came into the living room. He placed a hand on her shoulder but couldn't for the moment find any words of comfort.

"There's a message for you on the answering machine," she told him.

"Who is it?"

"Connolly, I think. He had a strange accent."

Niall played the message. The familiar nasal drawl of Gerry Connolly brought him winging back to when they'd sat at the same desk in Brunner and suffered the tender mercies of the Christian brothers. Once, for some minor infraction, Niall had been locked in a cupboard and begun to panic; it was Gerry who had risked the wrath of the teacher and let him out – and he paid dearly for it, at least six strokes of the leather. Shortly after that Gerry had organised an insurance policy for the kids in the class. The premium was sixpence a week and he paid out a half crown to anyone who got six or more slaps of the leather. He wasn't much of an actuary, however, and after a month he was bankrupt. But he was a good friend and never gave in to the grinding poverty of those days. Unfortunately his parents took him out of school when he was fourteen and put him into a succession of dead-end jobs. Niall wondered what he was doing in New York.

"Why don't you go and meet him?" Rona

said. "It would be a good break for you."

"I should do," he agreed. But he knew he wouldn't go to meet him because it would bring him back to that period of hopelessness in his life which he now realised was what had driven him into the seminary in the first place. He had opted for the safety and security of the institutional church and now, one turn of the circle later, he was back to despair. He had no way of knowing right then that in a matter of months he would seek Gerry Connolly out under quite different circumstances.

After their evening meal Niall made coffee and it was then that Rona decided to broach the subject.

"Diane has come up with some facts."

"Diane …? Oh, yes." He refused to say 'private investigator' and he noticed that Rona hadn't said it either. It was too ridiculous for words.

"She went to the breaker's yard and examined the car. She's sure it was hit from behind. The police didn't seem to be aware of that."

"A hit and run?" Niall raised his head until their eyes were on a level. It seemed strange to be discussing the matter of their daughter's death in such a detached way.

"She doesn't think so. There were signs that the car had been rammed. That would have been consistent with some … of the injuries."

"My god, are you suggesting that it was

deliberate?" It was inconceivable that Ros could have inspired dislike, much less hatred, in anyone. He loosened his tie with a sideways jerk and then undid the top button of his collar, but he still felt faint.

"There are a lot of sick people out there." Rona paused for breath; the recitation of such dire facts had taken its toll. "Motiveless crimes are on the increase."

"Christ, Rona, I don't know. I just don't know." He held his head, feeling the unsteady throb at the temples. It began to rain; through the French doors he could see the heavy drops hit the patio like squashed grapes. There was a menace of thunder in the air. There would be no possibility of gardening this evening, nothing to fill the dragging hours.

The next morning Niall awoke knowing there was something he had to do. He rang Si and told him he didn't need a lift. Then, following Rona's directions transmitted to sat nav, he drove to the breaker's yard which was like a mud bath after the thunderstorm the night before. The yard man got down from a tractor and asked him suspiciously what he wanted. Niall gave him the briefest particulars.

"There was a dame in here a few days ago looking at that car. A PI. You a cop? You don't look like a cop."

"No. Just … an interested party." Niall gave him a twenty dollar bill.

The man led him through a canyon between

mounds of old cars and trucks. His heart faltered when he saw the grey VW they'd bought for Ros just two years ago, insisting on a sturdy, reliable car. The back end was badly crumpled in at least three different places and the axle was definitely bent out of shape. The front was also damaged and showed signs of having hit the wall more than once. The roof and door columns were badly out of line. Niall was no engineer but that warping in the middle of the car suggested to him that the vehicle had been subjected to powerful forces to the front and back at the same time.

"It's been in the wars," the yard man said. "If you ask me no one got out of that alive."

Niall stared at his mud-stained shoes. He felt faint and was blinded by sunlight, reflected off the smashed glass and chrome of a thousand wrecks. Overwhelmed by that same sense of disorientation he'd experienced in the wood, he needed to lean against something or squat on the ground. He did neither but stayed on his feet, motionless, until his breathing became slightly easier.

As he drove away he remembered something the police had said. They'd received a call that night reporting an accident. The caller hadn't given his name. Why would a good Samaritan wish to conceal his name and if he had witnessed what actually happened why had he referred to it as an 'accident?

CHAPTER 7

DIANE SOAKED IN THE TUB listening to the Beatles. She was far too young to have experienced Beatlemania first hand but she liked their sound and the lyrics were good too. By contrast, the techno music of her generation, rap and hip-hop, left her cold; it was all so engineered and repetitive. The Lennon-McCartney melodies occasionally reminded her of the gospel music she'd loved as a teenager growing up in the outskirts of Atlanta.

When Rona Grenham had first walked into her small office in McLean – situated over a bookshop between ABC Liquor and Dart Drug – Diane had seen a non-case. They weren't that unusual and many non-cases were brought to her by women, operating on instinct or hunch or some felt need to do something to expiate a tragic event. Their money was of course as good as anyone else's. Diane normally took the non-case, anticipating that after a week at most she would advise the client to drop the matter. Usually, after a week or so she would have accumulated enough evidence to convince the client that the case was not worth proceeding with. To stretch it out beyond a week, or to mislead a client into thinking their suspicions were justified, would, however, be unprofessional. She had standards.

But four days into this case she realised that

Rona's suspicions were far from groundless and that the police had paid the matter scant attention. Diane doubted if professional criminals were involved and, other things being equal, that should make her job a bit easier. She needed whatever edge she could get. As a woman of colour in a white man's domain she had to establish credibility by building up a track record. Her younger sister was trying to get into art college by assembling a portfolio. Same thing really. Diane sometimes wondered if there ever came a time when you didn't have to prove yourself any more.

A few days ago, with the help of a yearbook, she had drawn up a list of Ros's classmates and had interviewed most of them. They were badly shaken by what had happened and seemed genuinely mystified by the suggestion that there could have been foul play. Ros hadn't stayed long at the graduation party and had spent most of that time helping out in the kitchen. She had come with a group from the *Gattopardo* in Georgetown and had left the party on her own, probably around eleven-thirty. Several other people had left before midnight; the party in fact had been a wash-out.

There were two people from that list whom Diane still had to contact. One was Gillian who, by all accounts, was Ros's closest friend. She was now working in Germany. Diane had a number for her but, after several attempts, still hadn't managed to track her down. The other person was Mark Highsmith.

With some reluctance Diane got out of the bath – where she did her best thinking – and had an early night. In the morning, immediately after a breakfast of bagels, cream cheese and coffee, she put through a call to Gillian and hit pay-dirt. It was a fraught conversation, however, and Diane felt relieved when it was over. She was sorry for the young woman who had lost her best friend and had not been able to attend the funeral. While there had not been a great deal of additional information, Diane at least knew what her next move had to be.

From the bay window David saw her coming up the path and thought at first that she might be a temporary replacement for his housekeeper, sent by the agency. He managed to keep his composure when Diane explained the reason for her visit and said she would like to put some questions to him.

"Of course," he said. "If there is anything I can do … Ros was a very special person and we are all devastated by her tragic death. I'm not really surprised by your visit. Niall told me they had engaged an investigator." He ushered her to an armchair where she sat with a notebook balanced on her knee. She began with some general questions about the neighbourhood and the relationships between both families then she gradually became more specific.

"…so you didn't hear about the tragedy until Sunday the 17th?"

"That's right. Two days afterwards." He noticed that her smile disappeared when she bent to her notebook. He badly needed a drink but didn't want to pour himself one in her presence. It annoyed him intensely that she had taken on the role of an authority figure. In the Embassy they would hardly trust her with the photocopying.

"And your son – Mark, isn't it? – had he seen her before that?"

"I don't know," he said carefully. He decided to have that drink after all; why should he be inhibited by her? And it was seven in the evening. He asked if she would like to join him but she declined. On resuming his seat, he balanced the glass on the arm of the chair. He touched it idly from time to time without drinking as if to indicate that its presence was of no consequence.

"But he would have seen her at the graduation party?" She looked at him with pencil poised.

"I don't think so." Keep it casual and vague, he thought, until he could establish how much she knew or thought she knew.

"I don't follow."

"Mark went to New York." David casually raised the glass of neat gin to his lips and confined himself to a delicate sip.

"He didn't go to the party? Why not?"

"He didn't graduate. Fell at the last fence so to speak."

"I'm confused," Diane said. "I'm almost sure some of the others saw him there." She made a point of leafing through the notebook. "Yes, four or five of his classmates said he was there."

David shrugged, "Now I'm confused … it's possible that he looked in." He tried to recapture that tone of professional detachment but it was becoming more difficult.

"But didn't you say he went to New York?" Diane's expression was one of self-deprecating puzzlement. She had often found that pose to be of use especially when interviewing men.

"He must have made a brief stop at the party on his way to the airport. That would square the circle." He tried to convey the impression that he was on her side, helping to explain things. "Yes, that was probably what happened. A token appearance."

"But he didn't come home here that night."

"No."

"You're sure?"

"Yes."

"And you mentioned the airport … Reagan … the Eastern shuttle I guess?"

"I would think so." Better, he thought, not to be too dogmatic. Leave himself some running room. In any case he certainly didn't want to create the impression that it was he who put his son on the plane.

"And he's still in New York?"

"Yes. He came back for the funeral of course but returned shortly afterwards."

"The funeral must have been traumatic for him."

"Very much so. Yes."

Diane said that it would be most helpful if she could talk to Mark at some stage and David had no option but to give her his phone number.

"One last question, Mr. Highsmith, if I may … what does Mark intend to do … careerwise?"

David's gorge rose. The cheek of the goddamn woman; this was none of her bloody business. "He's interested in the theatre." A complete fabrication though one he'd used before. As far as he was concerned Mark wasn't interested in anything except narcotics.

"A tough life."

"What?"

"Acting. The stage."

"Yes."

"Still, if he can make it there…"

"Quite … Now if there's anything else, don't hesitate…"

"Thank you, sir. You've been most helpful."

On the way out Diane looked again at the jeep in the carport. Was it her imagination or did the front grille and panel seem newer than the rest of the body?

It was much later when David finally got through to Mark, who was reasonably coherent, and told him to expect a call sometime in the near future, a call from a black woman, called Diane. Mark began by saying that he would refuse to talk to her. His father urged him to co-operate and he spent most of an hour rehearsing him on the line to follow. He could do no more.

CHAPTER 8

HAVING COMPLETED HIS VALUATION of the duplex apartments, Niall reckoned they were overpriced by about twenty percent on average; even those without a river frontage were above what the market would bear. He was glad he'd finished that part of the job in reasonable time because his powers of concentration had all but deserted him and he had to re-check his calculations and measurements more than usual. On presenting his conclusions, he was relieved when Jack Wyndham said he thought they made sense. The hard part still lay ahead, however: persuading the developer, Clive Norbert, to mark down his prices.

Niall didn't relish meeting Norbert again. The last time their paths had crossed had been at one of the annual picnics that were so dear to old Laughlin's heart. An old-fashioned entrepreneur, Laughlin liked to think that good business had to have some family dimension to it. He used his country club for the event; there were two swimming pools, several tennis courts, a special area for barbecues and the ubiquitous Budweiser truck. On this particular occasion he had also laid on pony rides for the kids.

A quantity surveyor from the Maryland office was just making his way back from the pony rides with his grandchildren when he suffered a heart attack and collapsed near to where the Grenham's were sitting.

Niall rushed to his side while Rona phoned for an ambulance and searched unsuccessfully for a defibrillator. Niall bent over the man and felt for a pulse in his neck. There was one, but it was faint. There was something odd about the man's breathing. Niall wanted to straighten him out but was afraid to move him in case of spinal injuries. The brief course he'd done in CPR was of little use to him in a real emergency. He looked around frantically for help. Rona indicated that the ambulance was on its way. But how long was it going to take? As Niall dithered and worried, Norbert, wearing Bermuda shorts, appeared from nowhere.

"Take his legs and lay him out flat. Quick!"

Niall and a bystander obeyed with alacrity. Norbert opened the man's mouth, fished out his dentures and peered in to see if there was any obstruction in the throat.

As if only just realising the gravity of the situation, Niall began whispering an Act of Contrition into the man's ear until Norbert told him to shut up and work on the chest instead. Finally, after a sudden voiding of the throat, the man started to breathe more easily.

As the paramedics were taking the man away, one of them turned to Niall and said,

"I think he'll make it. Good job."

"Good. Thank god. No, not me ... I just..."

He looked towards Norbert who shrugged and said, "What were you doing? Whispering sweet nothings in his ear? Jesus H. Christ."

So having been awed by Norbert's take-charge manner, Niall was bemused by the man's lack of subtlety. His bemusement turned to something more humbling when, on the way home, Ros asked from the back of the car what "sweet nothings" were.

"Dad helped save that man's life," Rona said.

"Not really." Niall was reluctant to pursue the conversation. "I did nothing." Then, under his breath, added, "As usual."

Negotiating had never been Niall's strong suit and as he walked into Norbert's expensively furnished office which reeked of cigar smoke, he felt defensive even before they got down to business. Norbert had a well-deserved reputation as a tough businessman; he had been around the block many times and had built his company from the ground up. He liked to boast that all of the sweat equity was his and his alone, but the fact was that he had asset-stripped a number of smaller companies along the way with scant regard for the jobs of those who worked in them.

"No foreplay," Norbert warned him. "Cut to the chase." Mercifully, he seemed to have forgotten the picnic incident.

Niall laid it out as best he could. Before he'd finished Norbert was shaking his head.

"No, no, no. Not a chance. It's a seller's market. You're two years behind the times."

"I don't think so," Niall said. "The units won't move at your prices…"

"Bullshit! Have you seen the recent auction results in Chevy Chase or Vienna or even that new development in Alexandria…?" He went on at length, throwing out anecdotes and self-serving stories as if they gave a definitive picture of market trends. His technique was to swarm all over the opposition and wear them down with bluster and selective corroboration. And it usually worked, proving that logic was no match for a forceful personality. Niall was already beginning to feel weary, as if his energy were being drained by Norbert's force-field. In the past he might have suggested a compromise but now, for some reason, he decided to make no concession. He might be intimidated but he wouldn't yield. He waited and waited until Norbert paused for breath and then he said in a mild voice, "None of that makes any difference. It's irrelevant."

This was so unexpected that instead of bringing up even heavier artillery, Norbert took a step backwards.

"Say what…?"

"We can all quote individual cases but the overall price index hasn't increased by more than 2 percent in the last year. And building costs have plateaued out."

"The index doesn't mean a damn thing," Norbert countered. "It's concocted by some fool bureaucrat who doesn't know his ass from page eight. I'm at the front edge." He hammered a finger against his sternum. "I know what's going on in the *REAL* world. The Republican camp followers are crazy about these kinds of apartments. They'll snap them up. For love nests, too. Passion hutches. Only yesterday one of the top White House guys bought a place in Rosslyn. The whole area is ready for gentrification." He continued to elaborate his worm's eye view of the market but Niall stayed on the high ground, finally stating, "We wouldn't be able to shift those units without a price cut of twenty percent."

"Sure you could, if you did the right kind of marketing." Norbert angrily stubbed out a half-finished cigar in an ashtray.

"The kind of marketing required would be prohibitively expensive. And it would be misleading. Both firms would lose goodwill. It's not on." This was the first time Niall had taken on Norbert and he found to his surprise that it wasn't as difficult as he'd imagined.

"You could take a cut in your commissions."

"No. They're pared to the bone as it is. It's your pricing structure that's out of line."

"You're not the only realtor in town," Norbert said darkly.

"That's true, but I think you'd find it difficult to get another firm to go for this package."

"Are you prepared to back that hunch?" Norbert asked him, biting off the end of another cigar and spitting it into a metal waste bin. It occurred to Niall that a cigar, more than anything else, symbolized a tycoon, and Norbert handled his in a slick and practiced manner.

"Yes." Niall knew this was the moment of truth but somehow it just didn't seem all that important. It was as if nothing concrete lay behind the drawings and the numbers they were discussing, no reality. It was all a game.

"Fine, that's fine. You're out of the loop boy. I'll have another firm on the job within the hour. On my terms. And I'm going to call Jack Wyndham and say you blew it." Norbert waved his arms around. "That's it. You've fucked the dog and won't even sell the pups. No more to be said. You know where the door is."

As Niall drove back along M Street it intrigued him how little the encounter had meant one way or the other. Whether they lost the business or Norbert finally came to heel was not a matter of great moment. In a strange way he felt liberated from such petty issues which, including his own life, could be viewed from a greater distance than before. There was nothing at stake any more since the worst had already happened.

Later that afternoon he remembered that Si had invited them to a reception at his business premises to introduce a new pastry chef – a real find apparently – to his clientele. When Niall received the invite his first instinct was to give it a miss. Now, however, he thought he might go along if Rona was agreeable.

"Why the change of heart?" Rona asked him when he picked her up at the corner of Eighteenth and M Street.

"Why not?" he said.

"Why not indeed?"

Si was like a fight promoter who'd got hold of a contender. He proudly introduced his new chef, whose most recent creations were on offer on buffet tables set up in the atrium of the building. Rona detached herself from Niall and joined Betty. Both of them studied and sampled the wide selection of canapés and pastries, then set about extracting trade secrets from the chef.

"Your sleuth gave me a grilling the other day."

Niall turned to see David, glass in hand, weaving his way towards him.

"Just going through the motions, I'm sure," Niall replied, a little uncomfortably. "Routine stuff I'd imagine."

"He hasn't called on me yet," Si put in as if he were disappointed.

"It's a 'she'," David said. "A woman of colour."

"A she? No kidding?" Si seemed impressed. "Why didn't she call on me?"

"You're just not that interesting." David changed the subject. "That new chef of yours. Only one thing wrong. Know what he calls these fancy comestibles? Finger food. Finger food, I ask you. Terrible use of the Queen's English." He swayed a little bit, holding his glass aloft like a torch. "And what about 'raw bar'? Awful expression, positively cringe-making."

Sensing an opportunity to put one over on him, Si remarked with a covert wink, "I thought today was one of your nooner days."

"Packed it in," David said. "Too old … Passed the big five-o last birthday. Got to hang the boots up sometime. Don't get me wrong. No need for Viagra. But the old libido's calmed down – 'mellowed out' as you might say."

"Christ, don't say that." Si looked personally offended. "I can't bear the thought."

David patted him on the shoulder. "You won't miss it, I promise you. A relief actually, not being in thrall to the old loins. Liberating in a way. One becomes serene, with a Zen-like control of the flesh…"

Rona interrupted to compliment Si on the quality of the cuisine, especially the angels on horseback and the bacon bouchées. Niall caught her eye to see if she wanted to leave but she seemed happy to stay longer and returned to Betty, who introduced her to some of the other guests.

"No," Si continued, "I don't like the idea of growing old at all. And it's not just the droops. My old man used to get up three or four times a night and could only manage a few dribbles. Prostate clapped out and the hormones all fucked up. It's not fair, you know, the loss of dignity."

"I'm sure there are compensations," Niall said.

"Yeah, smelling flowers or sitting in the park feeding crumbs to the pigeons." Si refused to be consoled. "I'm with W. C. Fields – life is a funny business; a man's lucky to get out of it alive."

"Well, as a great American philosopher once remarked, 'shit happens'." David delicately plucked another drink from a passing tray.

"I like the way you did that," Si observed. "A fluid movement of the arm, graceful like a conductor waving a baton."

"My right hand is automatically drawn to good champagne," David returned, "and, remember, I have more receptions under my belt than you've had hot dinners."

Half listening to the banter, Niall watched the sun going down behind the roof of the Treasury Building. It was a nice time of year. The humidity of summer had subsided like a fever breaking and the air had a softer, more spacious quality. This would be the last time the three of them would hang out together on one of those occasions where chewing the fat had no purpose beyond itself. And they might have stayed quite late if the wives had not intervened.

CHAPTER 9

IT TURNED OUT that Clive Norbert was successful in finding another firm of realtors to handle his property development on his terms. Although he tried to conceal his disappointment, Jack Wyndham did express his reservations when he walked into Niall's office.

"We'd have had these duplexes on our hands for at least a year," Niall pointed out. "Think of the overheads. And the effect on our reputation." He took a sip of his coffee and pushed it aside. It was much too strong and bitter for his taste but in six or seven years he had never mentioned this to the tea-lady.

"This new firm that Norbert's signed up … they obviously take a different view." Jack sat on the edge of the desk pursing his lips.

"It's a fairly new firm," Niall said. "They may be taking a loss-leader approach to gain a foothold. But I think they'll regret it. We're better off without that account." His secretary buzzed him to say his wife had been on the line and would like him to call her back.

Jack slid off the desk into one of the easy chairs and locked his fingers together in a prayer-like attitude. "I wonder if we shouldn't have seen it as a loss-leader? There might have been merit in keeping Norbert happy for the next deal and the one after that. Perhaps a longer-term view might have been taken."

Niall felt a tingling sensation in his scalp; he couldn't win for losing. Jack had an irritating habit of being wise after the event. "Norbert was always a bully," he said calmly. "And I think he'll get worse rather than better. We were going to have to cut bait at some stage."

"Hmmm." Jack looked far from convinced. "I wonder if he might know his segment of the market…"

"Better than I do?" Niall finished the sentence for him. "Look, Jack, you agreed with my valuation."

"On a cursory basis."

"So?"

"I didn't know you were going to go to the wire so quickly. I didn't know that." Jack looked crestfallen.

It occurred to Niall that they were two softies trying to have an argument without hurting any feelings in the process. It was like a pillow fight. The thought calmed him; in fact he felt a smile forming on his face. They were a pair of wimps.

"Do you think I handled the negotiations badly?" Again he had a quirky sense of giving his boss permission to criticise him.

"Well, I guess I didn't expect it of you." He consulted his fingertips. Then he stood up. "Oh look, let's not get into it now."

It was the slight emphasis on the word 'now' that assailed Niall's senses. It suggested that Jack was going easy on him because of his personal loss. And the subtlety of the implication made it all the worse. He was tongue-tied; when he looked up Jack had left the office. For a big man he moved quietly and quickly.

When he returned Rona's call she asked him to meet Diane and herself at a coffee shop in Georgetown at five o'clock. Niall asked for some more information but Rona suggested it would be better to wait until they met. The possibility that it might not have been an accident had weighed heavily on him, occupying his thoughts at every waking moment. He had tried to reason that the manner of Ros's death was of little significance compared with the brute fact that she was gone. The heart, however, did not make such distinctions and another layer had been added to the burden of grief.

He turned up at the coffee shop and found the two women waiting for him. They sat together at a round, marble-topped table on which Diane had placed a page of notes.

"Diane has a lot to tell us," Rona said, as if she were orchestrating a set piece or at least trying to avoid the idiocy of small talk. Diane took her cue, looking from one to the other.

"The last time we met we discussed the damage to your daughter's car and what it signified. I enlisted the help of a VW crash-test engineer to analyse the forces that the car was subjected to. Since then I've interviewed friends and acquaintances." With occasional references to her notes she described some of these, including the phone conversation with Gillian and the meeting with David Highsmith. For a moment Niall was distracted by the recollection of the mangled heap that had once been Ros's car. The twisted metal was the result of extraordinary violence; it was hard to imagine what would have caused such physical damage.

"So, having called Mark Highsmith, I went to see him in New York." Diane continued in a stilted monotone. "He is living in squalid conditions with a young woman, Sue Dreschler, who in my opinion is also addicted to controlled substances. Mark confirmed what his father told me. I then went to Reagan Airport and checked through the Eastern passenger lists with the help of a stewardess who owes me. Mark Highsmith was on a flight to New York on the morning of the 16th…" She paused. "But not until 9.30 a.m. …"

"I don't follow," Niall interjected. "As I understood it, Mark left on the night of the 15th. Or possibly in the early hours of the next morning…"

Diane nodded. "This is a major inconsistency."

Niall looked to Rona but she avoided his glance and continued to look down at her hands, folded in her lap. It seemed as if she had made her mind up about something.

"I'm sure there's a simple explanation," Niall said. "Did you follow it up?"

Diane hesitated, then said with finality, "I don't think we have to look any further."

"But…" Niall had to lean to one side as the waitress arrived with the coffee. The discussion, which began to chill him to the bone, was put on hold until the waitress went away.

"You should be aware," Diane continued, "that the front of Mr. Highsmith's jeep has been repaired recently. And the man who reported the 'accident' spoke with a British accent."

"What … are you saying…?" Niall asked. He began to see but it was too sudden to be grasped at once. Rona at least had probably had a forewarning. "…that David…?"

"No, not the father," Diane cut in. "Mark." She paused for breath. "There is no doubt in my mind that Mark Highsmith drove your daughter off the road, using that jeep, and caused her death … I'm sorry if this comes as a further shock to you." She remained silent for as long as it took, and her sense of personal victory waned as she contemplated the pale, stunned faces across the table. While in New York, Sue Dreschler had followed her out of the flat and, in exchange for a hundred dollars, told her that Mark had mentioned Ros's name in his sleep. Because a bribe was involved Diane decided not to present that evidence; it was in any case unnecessary.

"Deliberately?" Niall asked at length. "Deliberately?"

Diane answered carefully. "Drugs were involved and there may have been … some clouding of judgement. But, in the normal meaning of the word, I would have to say it was deliberate. Yes."

"For god's sake, why?" Niall's hands cupped his mouth as if he were about to get sick. Rona grasped his shoulder as if to apologise for the shock which she had sprung on him and which she had had a longer time to process.

"My guess would be that he felt jealous of Ros, of her success and of the fact that she had outgrown him. Jealousy and drugs can be a lethal combination. According to two of the people at the party, he made a pass at Ros and she rejected him. It wasn't anything serious," she added hastily, "but he probably read too much into the rebuff."

After a long, dazed silence Niall asked whether David was implicated in any way. Diane told him that in her opinion he had alibied his son from the very beginning. Niall's mind began to race. He gripped the edge of the table and eventually found Rona's comforting hand.

Diane felt obliged to enter an important caveat. "Of course, all of this is circumstantial. I don't think it would stand up in court." She had to make this point because in her experience most clients assumed that ordinary facts were legal facts whereas there was a world of difference between them.

"How much proof do we need?" Rona asked in a trembling voice.

"I'll be honest with you," Diane said. "I could investigate this for years and we'd probably be no further along legally speaking. There were no witnesses at the scene of the crime, and it would be hard to establish a solid motive. Remember that proving guilt beyond a reasonable doubt is a very demanding standard. I doubt if the DA's office would go for it." It would also be impossible, she thought, to get Sue Dreschler to testify and she would be a very flaky witness anyway.

"But we have to involve the police now." Rona looked towards her husband for some kind of support but he seemed a million miles away.

"The trail's gone cold," Diane said. "They wouldn't give it priority at this stage, especially without witnesses. You could try the Grand Jury route. But if you ask my opinion, I don't think anything short of a confession would work."

Knowing that Diane was right accentuated Niall's sense of bewilderment. Ros was deliberately murdered by that sick bastard who skipped off to New York, alibied by his father who had … what? … yes, become more distant in the last three or four months. It all made sense now … murder and collusion … Jesus Christ. A spark jumped from grief to anger.

Rona was weeping silently, clutching his hand. Diane put the notes back into her briefcase, offered sympathies and made a diplomatic exit. She hated when cases like this one were relatively easy to solve and yet were not prosecutable; she felt as if she had failed her clients.

"What are we going to do?" Niall asked after a while.

"I don't know … We need more evidence." Her throat was dry. "But the police are not going to help."

"Or a confession," he reminded her.

"Some hope."

"You were right all along."

Rona didn't answer. She felt drained, beaten to a pulp. Maybe there were no answers.

CHAPTER 10

APART FROM A HANGOVER Mark was in tolerable shape when his father paid him a visit on the Saturday. He introduced him to Sue who, had just thrown on some clothes when she heard the bell ring. David took in the dreadful room, its peeling plaster and exposed pipework, with one disdainful glance. He could tell immediately that Sue was a user and that she and Mark were an unholy alliance, formed to feed a mutual habit. Having stood for a while, awkwardly, under the sloping roof he sat, when invited, on the bed that took up most of the floor space.

"To what do we owe the pleasure?" Mark inquired with a ghastly attempt at a pleasantry.

"Oh, just passing through," David answered vaguely. "So, how is the new job going?"

"Fine," Mark said. "It keeps the wolf from the door … for the time being. We work together," he added, with a nod in Sue's direction.

"I see … I see." It was a shock to find Mark in such a squalid state; he remembered him as a kid, clean-cut and neat in his habits. He even used to fold his pyjamas and put them carefully on a shelf in his wardrobe. When had the fatal derailment occurred? Sometime after his mother's death? She had doted on him, of course, and it must have shocked him at some level of consciousness when she suddenly disappeared from his life.

"Would you like some coffee, Mr. Highsmith?" Sue asked.

"No thank you. I just had some." He wondered how on earth she would make it. All he could see was one dirty saucepan on the gas ring in the corner. Despite her sickly grin he could see she was one tough bitch, trailer-park material. She was obviously no good for Mark but he also knew that his son was canny enough not to get entangled long-term with such a creature.

The conversation, such as it was, dragged on for a while, then Sue said she had some grocery shopping to do and made good her escape.

Because of their last fraught encounter David had resolved to play it cool, but as soon as the door closed he gave vent to his dismay.

"Christ, Mark, this is the pits."

"What do you mean?" Mark feigned innocence but there was an edge to his voice.

"This pigsty…" He was going to include Sue in his general condemnation but thought better of it. "Do you not see how low you've sunk?"

"Money doesn't grow on trees."

"The problem is, if I give you more money you'd become even more addicted. Don't you see…?"

"What are you talking about? I'm clean. I haven't touched the stuff for ages."

"Do you expect me to believe that?" David

thought of all the lies he'd heard, those senseless, outrageous denials. And yet he wanted to believe them, hoped against hope.

"Believe what you like." Mark gave a slow shrug. "I'll fight my own battles. I always have … without any support from you or anyone else."

David had encountered this long-suffering act before and although he saw it for what it was, he still felt a spasm of guilt. Where was the real Mark behind all these poses? He wasn't going to find out on this flying visit. Maybe he never would. Surprisingly, the thought did not distress him unduly.

"Did that private investigator contact you?"

"Yeah, some black dame called here asking all kinds of questions."

"She came here … in person?"

"Sure did. Walked straight in without a bye or leave. Nosey bitch. Made herself right at home."

Her own apartment was probably infinitely better than this one, David thought. "And you told her what we agreed?"

"I stuck to the script if that's what you mean. What's it all about anyway?"

"Wha-a-t?" David looked at him in consternation.

"Why was she asking me all those questions?"

"You know that Ros Grenham is dead…?"

"Of course I know that. There was this awful

car accident. I was at the funeral, remember?"

"Wait now…" David tried to clear his head. Maybe the sordidness of the place was affecting him. Was it conceivable …? "What are you telling me? Are you saying you weren't … involved in the accident?"

"Christ, you know and I know that I was here in New York when it happened. I was shocked when I heard about it. Poor Ros…" He was so matter-of-fact that David began to wonder if he had blocked it out or else was suffering from a drug-related dysfunction. In either event some action was called for but he didn't know what. He might have to think about some form of medical intervention. On the other hand, if Mark did believe what he'd just said it would be hard for any investigator to break him down. Or the law for that matter. He wasn't sure if he'd just discovered a silver lining or an even darker cloud.

He looked at the wretched face in front of him – still young but on the verge of ruin – and could fathom nothing of what lay behind the blank surface of the eyes.

PART II

CHAPTER 11

THE BALL STARTED well, on a low and rising curve; then for no apparent reason it began to leak right, and further right as if in the grip of some invisible power – the golfer's nemesis.

"Ah shit," Si said under his breath as he watched the ball land on the next fairway over. To add insult to injury it kicked right viciously – ending up in the rough on the wrong hole.

"You really sliced that one," Betty observed.

"Oh really? Further right than Attila and Hun. I should've faded it," Si said as if he could produce a fade at will. He fiddled with his grip and took a practice swing, trying to moderate his sometimes excessive hip shimmy.

"You're meant to do that before you hit the ball, not afterwards," Betty pointed out with a sideways grin towards Rona. Si walked with them towards the ladies' tee and waited impatiently. It seemed to him that they spent more time adjusting their dress than addressing the ball. Both drives were miserable daisy-cutters and the two women laughed shamelessly. He set off smartly towards the next fairway, making apologetic gestures to the golfers who were playing that hole. Maybe he should have quit after nine holes like Niall had done.

"Don't mind him," Betty said. "He takes it very seriously. Some men are fanatics about this game."

"Not Niall though," Rona replied. It was a good while since they'd played together and she liked Betty's company. They walked on, took their next shots, talking as they did. They could see Si in the distance trying to take a short-cut across a stream. He gave up after a while and headed for the stone bridge.

"I can relax a bit now," Rona said. "Things have eased up a little at work."

"I don't know how you do it," Betty said. "You have to select the lines, negotiate with the suppliers, arrange displays ... and take responsibility for large expenditures. I couldn't do it..." She topped her next shot and the ball squirted about twenty yards. Neither woman made any comment; quality of shot was a matter of supreme indifference to them.

"Of course you could. It's not so difficult. After a few years' experience your confidence grows."

Betty shook her head. "Not for me. I wouldn't be able to hack it."

"Remember, it's teamwork too. And women are good at that. There are also safety valves in every job..." Rona used a three wood and made good contact with the ball which had a fluffy lie.

"Safety valves? I don't follow."

"Well, whenever you make a poor decision you usually find a safety valve or a way out of it. For example, one year a particular line of skirts didn't do very well. So we put them on offer and moved about half that way. I was still pretty embarrassed though and talked it over with the suppliers. They took them back at cost on condition that I'd give them an order the following year. Problem more-or-less solved. Another time we went very up-market with outer wear. Real classy stuff. The margins were great but turnover fell. So we bought in cheaper merchandise from Taiwan to give a better balance. That helped a bit. There are always safety valves. Most jobs would be impossible without them."

When Rona had started out all those years ago in the millinery department her ambition was to move to the cosmetics department but she knew she wasn't pretty enough. So she went to night school and studied cost accounting. But even then she had no idea she would become the senior fashion buyer; it seemed completely beyond her reach. Now, incredibly, she was beginning to weary of it. The colours of her world had begun to fade like some of the stone-washed fabrics she dealt in.

"I still think you did extraordinarily well in combining career and home. And neither suffered."

"I hope not." Rona played her approach shot. Although she boned it, the ball skittered through a bunker and made the apron of the green.

From the next fairway over Si tried to drill a two iron through a copse of trees. They heard the sound of foliage being shredded, the thunk of ball on bark, followed by a strangled cry.

"Ros was a wonderful girl ... wonderful," Betty said. "She was a credit to you." Tears came to her eyes. Though childless, she had some sense of the pain involved.

"She had it front and centre from the word go," Rona responded. "We just stood back and let her develop..." And how she had developed. There was that occasion when Rona discovered that one of her agents was sourcing textiles from sweatshops in Indonesia where the workers were paid the equivalent of two dollars a day. Rona's first instinct was to pull the plug. Everyone she discussed it with had a different angle on it, or an axe to grind. Ros posed one question: "What would the workers want?" And that was the line Rona followed up, discovering that the workers were satisfied with their wages and that the politically correct solution would not have appealed to them at all. Ros had such good instincts, so much to offer. Why, why?

"Has the investigator turned up anything?" Betty asked.

"Not much." Rona regretted that she had to be less than frank. "It looks like it may have been a hit and run..."

"Oh my god. That's awful ... truly awful." With an indifferent approach shot Betty managed to get on the edge of the green. She always felt safe when that happened because there were no more long and unpredictable shots. With any luck she'd be down in three or four putts. From across country Si was converging on the green, having given himself a free drop out from behind a staked tree.

"It must be tough on Niall too," Betty added.

"Yes. He doesn't show it and he won't hear about counselling. I'm not sure what's going on inside…"

"When Si's mother died two years ago he didn't shed a tear. He busied himself with the arrangements. He did it all on his own. He even kept on with those silly jokes right through the funeral. He just wouldn't let it out, not if his life depended on it."

Rona noticed the sun going down behind a belt of sitka spruce that formed the western perimeter of the course. A young deer stuck its nose out of the dense foliage, sniffed the air and retreated with a kick of its hind legs.

" And I don't think it's just a macho thing," Betty was saying. "I think that most men respond to things in a more complex way than we give them credit for."

"I wonder?" It was true that Niall had become more withdrawn and she didn't quite know how to cope with that. For her part she had achieved some kind of 'closure', as the counsellors termed it. She now accepted that she would never see Ros again and that became the focus of her grief.

For some reason she doubted if Niall had reached any such conclusion but she couldn't be sure. Without a focus had he any single, coherent goal to work towards? She suspected he was floundering badly.

She was almost sorry now that she'd hired Diane. Where had it got them? A little further along perhaps but straight into a cul de sac. And they had to live in the same neighbourhood as the Highsmith's, pretending they knew nothing. One of the many difficult questions they were left with was the extent of the blame attaching to David for trying to protect his son. How were they supposed to deal with that?

"Hey, you're in my peripheral vision," Si complained as he bent over his ball.

"Oh, just putt. Don't take it so seriously," Betty replied.

"Shadow … shadow." He waved them away with his hand.

They moved again to a different spot on the green while he white-knuckled the putter. He was a little too diffident and the ball stopped on the very lip of the hole.

He stared at it for a long time and then said, "Sweet Jesus."

"Si!" Betty upbraided him.

"It's a prayer, a prayer. This damn game is too frustrating. I haven't the temperament for it." He studied his card with resurgent hope. "If I can par the short one and hit the greens in regulation I could still finish under ninety, gross…" The *ifs* of golf.

On the next hole, a par three, Si got lucky and nailed the ball on the green, pin high. He even got a little back spin which, though a pure fluke, pleased him greatly.

"What club did you use?" Betty inquired.

"Now you know you mustn't ask that," Si responded. "A golfer may volunteer that information but it is wrong to ask. Protocol, you see." As he put the club back in his bag Betty made a point of looking at it.

"A six iron, huh."

This time all three players were more or less together as they walked down the short fairway.

"That's ground under repair," Betty said as she found her ball.

"Let me check." Si examined the terrain and consulted the rules on the back of his card. "OK, a drop. Not nearer the hole. One club length…" He broke off in consternation as he saw her kicking the ball out of the rough. "Wh-a-a-t …? Christ, you can't do that … That's a penalty of two strokes."

"Forget it." With the toe of her shoe she improved her lie further. "Who's counting?"

"We must have rules," he said sternly. "Otherwise it's anarchy…" He spread his hands in a gesture of hopeless abandon.

"And this from a man," Betty said, "who tries every trick in the book to keep hygiene inspectors away from his kitchens."

"That's different. If I poison people I'll pay the price. Me. What do we need inspectors for? Paper-pushers the lot of them. Anyway that's business. This is golf."

Niall lay on a lie-low near the pool, wrapped

in white towels like an Egyptian mummy. Even though the sun wasn't very hot there could still be harmful rays filtering through the ozone layer. He didn't tan well anyway. A standard fair-skinned Celt who hadn't yet acquired that honeyed American pigmentation. But he could swim well despite his one-time terror of water. The reason he had taken steps to conquer his fear was, not untypically, due to an even greater fear. When Ros was young he used to have morbid fantasies in which she was struggling in deep water, on the point of drowning. The question his imagination posed for him was whether he would have the guts to dive in and save her. He hoped like hell that he would do the right thing but he just couldn't be sure. He agonised over this purely fictional dilemma and often had terrifying nightmares about it. Finally, he signed up for swimming classes and, though it took several weeks before he would even put his face in the water, he eventually learnt to swim. But that wasn't enough because the better he became the more severe were the hypothetical tests he set for himself. It was only when he earned his diploma for life-saving – which he displayed on the wall of the bedroom – that he began to relax. So, he had conquered that fear – only to have it replaced by a far worse reality.

Having spent some time on the nineteenth hole, Si arrived home in good form with the other golfers and proceeded to fire up the barbecue in the back yard. As the steaks spattered on the grill a swarm of fireflies appeared, attracted by the smell of burning fat and hickory-wood smoke that curled up into the encroaching dusk. The guttural sounds of cicadas and tree frogs gave a tropical feel to the night.

CHAPTER 12

AS HE SAT in the front room waiting for his lift, Niall looked out the bay window wondering if the hedges needed trimming. It was years since he had done a proper job on the garden. Ros, who was about seven at the time, had been fascinated by the unaccustomed burst of activity and had helped put the clippings into black plastic sacks. It must have been a Saturday because that was the day Fairfax County provided a free refuse disposal service. He had dumped all of the sacks into the back of the station wagon he drove then and driven with Ros to Balls Hill Road where the refuse trucks waited to receive the plunder of all the once-a-year gardeners who lined up behind them.

After Niall threw the sacks into one of the trucks he started to drive out of 'trash heaven', as he called it, much to Ros's amusement. It was only then that he saw the waiting squad cars hidden behind the trucks. The police were out in force, checking licences, county stickers and decals. Niall, who was wearing shorts and tee-shirt, did not have his driver's licence on him and that in itself was an offence. He was led to a squad car and told to sit in the back. Other mild-mannered suburbanites were also sequestered. It was ludicrous and ham-fisted but Niall did not complain until he saw Ros's face pressed against the window of his own car several yards away.

She was crying, on the verge of hysteria, assuming that her father had been arrested and would be driven away. He made to get out of the squad car but found that both of the back doors had locked automatically.

"I have to go to my daughter..." he said to the young cop in the front seat.

"Stay where you are," the cop admonished him.

"You don't understand ... she's scared..." His voice went higher as his own anxiety grew.

"Just hold it, buddy."

Niall experienced real panic during the few minutes it took for the cop to write the ticket and when he did get back to Ros she was in a bad state. She clung to him all the way home and when she eventually recovered he tried to explain to her that he wasn't being arrested, that it was merely a technicality. She wanted to know what a technicality was and he told her it was something which had to be done even though it was of no importance. His main concern had been for her, but he couldn't deny a more unworthy thought. Had he been humiliated in her eyes? Her all-powerful Dad held captive by a young cop, still wet behind the ears.

It was Si who told him years later that the police were probably doing a favour for the Mafia, who wanted a monopoly on the refuse disposal business. Although Niall wasn't convinced of that, he lost respect for the police – a view which more recent events did nothing to alter. The experience, minor enough in retrospect, also made him more alert to the possibility of sudden and capricious dangers, though not, he now realised, alert enough.

From the bay window he saw David guide the jeep into the driveway to collect him. As soon as he sat into one of the rear seats, David reversed and headed for Kirby Road. Si was in the passenger seat reading the *Post*, and trying, as he put it in Air Force jargon, to amalgamate the faeces. All three were slow starters on a Monday morning, so there was little conversation. Niall broke the silence by saying, "I see you got some work done on the front of the jeep."

"Oh … yes," David said lightly. "I didn't know you … had an eye for that kind of thing."

"I'm fairly observant at times." Niall swallowed bile that came to his throat. He sensed that a new phase was beginning, one that couldn't be reversed, maybe not even controlled.

"I didn't notice anything." Si looked up briefly from his paper. "Did you hit something?"

"Took a bend too fast some time ago and hit … a tree. It was stupid really." David merged on to the parkway and stayed in the slow lane.

"It must've been some impact to damage this monster." Si slapped the dashboard.

"I suppose I'd had a drink or two," David said ruefully. Admitting to a minor infraction was good for credibility, he thought.

"Why didn't you mention it before now?" Si asked.

"I … why?"

"I know a terrific panel beater. Started out servicing aircraft in Dulles, then set up on his own. Cheap too. I could've put you in touch with him."

"Maybe next time. Should a tree get in my way again."

"It didn't look like a panel-beating job to me," Niall said quietly.

"They may have put in some new parts." David shrugged. "I'm no mechanical genius." He slowed down to let a Corvette change lane in front of him. It had taken him years to appreciate that when a Virginian driver flashed an indicator he wasn't asking for permission to change lane; he was going to do it. David used to pull a horse box with the jeep when Mark had a pony. He recalled with some surprise how Mark had cared for that animal, sometimes sleeping with it in the stable. He seemed to have preferred that to slumber parties and scout meetings. The pony probably meant more to him than his best friend. Who was his best friend then? Ros. God, so it was. Whatever became of the pony? They must have sold it but David couldn't remember being involved in the transaction. Maybe Mark had sold it himself but if so what had he done with the money? Did he really have to ask?

"It looks like a good job," Niall was saying. "Which garage did you bring it to? The one at the corner of Old Kirby?"

"What? Oh, I don't know … I gave it to one of the drivers at the embassy. He looked after it for me."

"Oh-ho, got the hired help to take care of it, did we, Lord Snot? You diplomats are something else." Si wagged his head and returned to his newspaper. His method of smoothing out creases in the paper was to give a few vicious jerks to the edges and hope for the best. Sometimes the creases snapped out; sometimes he was left holding shreds of newsprint in his hands, with the bulk of the paper lying crumpled in his lap. Occasionally he marked an article with a felt pen; presumably, he would cut it out later. No one knew for sure. The items probably related to catering or golf because he wasn't particularly well up on world affairs. Where TV was concerned he tended to watch the celebrity chefs – and at one stage considered the possibility of trying to become one.

"Mark has been away for a long time now," Niall remarked.

David caught his eye in the rearview mirror. "He likes New York. Mind you, he's only waiting on tables but it may be the chance he needs, you know, to … find his niche, or whatever they say nowadays."

"We haven't seen much of him," Niall said.

"He didn't stay long at the funeral. I know that he and Ros were good friends. I hope he's not taking it too badly." He kept his eyes focused on the mirror.

"I imagine … Well, you know what he's like. Not very demonstrative … it all goes inside." David looked straight ahead. "The apple doesn't fall far from the tree." He shrugged. Genes, heredity; we were all creatures of a prevailing science. Determinism could excuse a lot. What the hell was this inquisition all about?

"Rona's meeting that investigator again today," Niall said. "She's got a lead apparently."

"Really?"

Si also looked up; the paper slid off his lap. "A lead?"

"Yes."

"I'd imagine…" David started slowly, "you'd have to be careful with … people like that … To make sure they're not in it just for the money. I mean they could easily exploit clients who are in a vulnerable situation. I can understand Rona's need of course. Don't take this the wrong way. But would she not be better off with a counsellor?"

"Do you think so?" Niall asked, fighting to control his anger.

"Just a thought." On that modest note the conversation died.

At the embassy David's assistant told him that the third quarter's balance-of-payments figures showed a deterioration way beyond what the markets had been expecting. It was bound to mean a hike in interest rates which would cause a dead cat bounce in equities and a bloodbath in the bond market. She had become as feverish and predictable as the language of the market place. David sent her off to cobble together a note for Whitehall. Even though her assessment was infantile it was probably correct because the barrow boys who traded securities around the world were also infantile. Two wrongs made it right and that's why idiots made money. They got the message off by ten thirty and that was his day's work done.

The conversation in the jeep had unsettled him and he didn't relish the prospect of the ride home that evening. Still, Niall couldn't suspect anything. He was rather a simple soul, even a little naive. He put the matter out of his mind. Just before lunch he called a friend who worked with the UN in New York and told him he was worried about Mark and would appreciate it if somebody would check on him from time to time. Stress, that sort of thing.

Jack Wyndham continued to sulk. It still bothered him that Niall had not consulted him before presenting Norbert with a *fait accompli*. Niall left him to his own devices but he was disappointed in him, as were the other executives. Jack had had his honeymoon period in charge of the firm and was now being judged by his peers. The verdict – a whispered one – was that he was out of his depth. He had the smarts but not the intestinal fortitude. Niall wondered vaguely what they would have said about him if he had landed the top job. He doubted if he would have got off as lightly as Jack Wyndham since, with one recent exception, he didn't find it easy to make decisions.

Oddly enough, Clive Norbert called him one morning and they had almost finished their conversation before Niall realised that he had been offered a job. It turned out that Norbert had been impressed by him, or at least, to his amazement, claimed to have been. He called him a stubborn Irish mule – which was an original way of trying to recruit someone. Niall turned him down, of course. Perhaps it was a joke, but in any case the thought of working for Norbert was far worse than the actuality of working for Wyndham. Far from being miffed by Niall's rejection of his offer, Norbert went into conciliatory mode, cracked a few crude jokes and ended by re-hiring the firm to handle his duplex development at Rosslyn. He seemed keen to give the impression that he was a big enough man to take a few knocks in his stride.

Jack Wyndham was elated when he heard the good news. "You did it, Niall. You got him back on board. And on your terms. Way to go."

"He probably couldn't hack it with a

different firm," Niall began, uncomfortable with the adulation.

"That's beside the point," Wyndham insisted. "You crowded him, cut him off at the knees. Norbert of all people."

"Jack, don't go on about it," Niall said. "It could have gone one way or the other. It was fifty-fifty all along the line…"

"You called it right."

"No, I didn't. Don't you see? I just called it one way. And that way just happened to turn out right in the end. It was pure happenstance." Niall had an urge to get out of the office, away from the cloying praise of his mercurial boss. Was there a building site he needed to visit? He had an urge to mix cement with a shovel, to be with men who did hard physical work in the open air.

"What's the matter? I'm trying to congratulate you." Wyndham looked as befuddled as he sounded.

"You were upset when you thought I'd lost the account. Now, suddenly, everything is fine. It's pure chance. I don't want to be judged on the basis of chance." Niall was conscious of sounding priggish but it had to be said.

"Chance is part of life." Wyndham spread his hands in a gesture of cosmic affinity. He, at least, was not going to be done out of his celebratory mood. As he went down the hall he could be heard telling the good news to all and sundry.

"Chance…" Niall repeated to himself. He stabbed the blotter pad on his desk with a bamboo paper knife and contemplated the little pock marks.

When he got home that evening Rona had the coffee ready.

"Do you know Congressman Naylor?" she asked him as they sat at the kitchen table.

"I think I bumped into him once or twice. Why?"

"We should ask him to try for a grand jury investigation."

"Will it do any good?" He remembered that Diane had been fairly dismissive of that option and he was inclined to trust her judgement. Besides, he hadn't much faith in the political process.

"You're not exactly supportive," Rona said a little stiffly.

"I don't know much about the procedure, the rules of evidence ... But I have the feeling it probably wouldn't..."

"But you know that son of a bitch is guilty..."

"I know it."

"Then we have to do something..." She turned to face him. "Why are you hesitating? He killed Ros ... You know it and I know it. Don't you want justice ... for her sake?" She brought a napkin to her face and used it roughly to dry unwanted tears.

"We're on the same side," he said gently. He went to make a couple of sandwiches. They rarely sat down to a meal any more. The vacant chair was too obvious a reminder. He buttered the bread and got some cold cuts from the fridge. Keep your enemies close, he thought, though he had no idea where the phrase came from.

"I think we should invite David to dinner later in the week," he said.

"Are you crazy?"

"Maybe." There was an unaccustomed pulse beat in his neck.

Later he went out to the garden and made some desultory passes over the grass with the mower. Whenever he approached the front boundary he had a view of David's house. It was silent and shuttered as usual.

CHAPTER 13

BECAUSE SI OFTEN had to work weekends he valued the leisure that this particular Saturday offered. He lay in a hammock slung between two apple trees, a glass of iced tea balanced on a stomach which was not quite as flat as he thought. Betty sat in a white-painted wicker chair, reading the recent issue of the 'Smithsonian' that had an interesting article on the growing market in dinosaur bones which were regularly being discovered in the mid-western States.

"I don't think so," she repeated, laying the magazine aside.

"What?" Si opened his eyes which had been beginning to close. He was momentarily startled by the cobalt blue of the sky and by the chill of the cold glass on his stomach. Some drops of condensation had gathered in his navel.

"I don't think they're back to normal. Rona and Niall. Not by a long shot."

It's too soon," he said. "Give them time." He struggled to keep his eyes open. There were two kinds of sleep, necessary and lazy; he was in the grip of the latter and abandoning himself to that luxury, which was, he reflected, almost as good as sex.

Betty shaded her eyes against the sun. She knew that tragedy could bring people closer or drive them apart but rarely, if ever, could the status quo ante be maintained.

"I feel uneasy with them. And it shouldn't be like that. They're good friends. It's my fault … are you listening to me?" She raised her voice.

"Don't beat yourself up. It's the situation not the people." He was more awake now; not even the gentle sway of the hammock could return him to the verge of sleep. "I'm walking on eggshells too."

"What do you mean?"

"Well, the car pool. Conversation not as easy as before. I don't know what to say half the time. Try the odd joke. Usually bombs. And the atmosphere between the other two…"

"What about it?"

"You know." He described some vague shape with his hands.

"I don't know. That's why I'm asking." She got up, walked towards one of the apple trees and looked down at him.

"It's sort of a recent thing. Niggly, I guess. I can't describe it…"

"Try, lover. Take it one step at a time. Is it personal?"

"What? Between Niall and David?"

"No. The man in the moon." Her expression, which loomed over his face, gave him no quarter.

"I'm not sure." He half-raised himself on an elbow. "Yeah, maybe there's something in that. Like, pleasant on the surface but something else going on underneath." He looked up at her to see if that was enough. She seemed satisfied for the moment and went back to her chair though not the magazine.

It was much later in the day when she hazarded an opinion that was close to the mark.

"You've been in the sun too long," Si replied. "It was an accident, one godawful, terrible accident. These things happen."

"Think about it."

"Christ, Betty. This is Loch Raven for god's sake. Normal, boring, everyday suburbia. No loose cannons on deck out here. We're all burbed out and buttoned down. It's your imagination." He sat up, his legs dangling over the edge of the hammock. "And Niall … you think he could keep up a charade like that? Niall of all people. You're kidding."

The last point gave Betty pause for thought, but she wouldn't abandon her theory just yet, not just yet.

Si was not particularly gracious in what he perceived as victory. "Niall, Hah. That's rich. Get real." He refilled his glass from the pitcher of iced tea.

When she answered her mobile phone and heard the proposition Julie started to laugh. It was outrageous.

"You can't be serious." She was in a shopping mall and people began to look at her, some smiling faintly as if echoing her laughter. Instinctively, she turned away and found herself facing the window of a boutique.

"I am serious," David said.

"Look, you're the one who broke off our … relationship, not me. Now you come along and suggest … what? … a date? For god's sake, it's too good to be true. Can't you find someone else to take to the prom?"

"There's no one else," David said. "I don't socialise much, you know that. Come on, Julie, be a sport. I'll make it up to you … For old times' sake."

"Cut out the bullshit. Why can't you go on your own? It's only dinner in a neighbour's house."

"The invitation specified a 'friend'." In fact he had wondered about that. Normally Rona was quite happy to have him along on his own so she could do a little matchmaking. He wasn't quite sure why this invitation was different. Of course he didn't want to go at all but he couldn't very well refuse. At the very least he wanted someone else to be present as a foil or distraction, anything to take the spotlight off him. From the word go he had dismissed the idea of bringing Mark.

Julie eventually agreed on the basis of a top-line escort fee.

On the evening in question she arrived by cab to his house, wearing a rather brief miniskirt that clung to her hips.

"Like the gear?" she inquired with a grin.

"Very fetching," he said. Was she showing him what he was missing or trying to make him out to be a sugar daddy? He was not unduly concerned either way, nor about the fact that she looked a little cheap.

"You're both very welcome," Rona said when they arrived. She ushered them into the sitting room, then excused herself and went back to the kitchen while Niall seated them around a coffee table laden with snacks and drinks.

After a while Julie went into the kitchen and asked Rona if there was anything she could do to help.

"No thanks," Rona said. "It's all done now. I was just putting the finishing touches to the rack of lamb." She still had serious reservations about the evening but Niall had been unusually keen. They returned to the sitting room.

In a conversational, almost offhand tone, Niall told them that lamb had been Ros's favourite dish. In the silence that followed Julie looked at him blankly. There was no elaboration. Niall didn't say anything. David realised that he should have put her in the picture beforehand. He had no option now but to explain the situation to her which he did in a halting monotone, concentrating on the bare facts.

"Oh, I'm sorry. I'm so sorry…" Julie went pale beneath her make-up.

"What's done can't be undone," Niall said. "We have to get on with our lives. That's the

American way." In an aside he told his wife that Betty and Si would not be coming; they had called earlier to cancel. He apologised for not having told her sooner. Her look of disbelief changed to one which indicated that a steward's inquiry would be held later. In a barely disguised tone of disinterest she asked her guests how they had met.

"Well, we've known each other for some time," Julie said.

"You could say we're old friends," David added a little uncomfortably.

Rona passed the pretzels around and offered to recharge the glasses. "And you never told us you had such an attractive friend … Still waters…" There followed the first of many excruciating silences.

Sometime later, Julie's attention was drawn to a young beech tree in the garden, visible through the French doors. It was swaying alarmingly and she pointed to it.

"Don't worry about that," Niall said. "There's probably a racoon in the tree. It happens a lot. They don't do any harm."

"It's wonderful out here in Virginia," Julie enthused, glad to have a subject of conversation. "You could be in the heart of the country and yet it's only, what? six or seven miles outside Washington. You have the best of all worlds…" She tailed off, biting her lip. "And the house is so fine and spacious."

"Too big for us now," Niall said.

"Why?" Julie suddenly realised. "On yes, of course … of course … I'm sorry."

Rona invited them to move into the dining room where they sat around the oval table. Julie, who now regretted the brevity of her skirt, was relieved to get her legs out of sight. To make assurance doubly sure she spread the napkin across her knees.

When they finished the chowder, the ingredients of which were discussed at length, Niall brought in and served the lamb. Rona laid the vegetables on the table and passed the mint sauce around.

"How is the job going?" David dabbed at his moustache with a napkin to make sure none of the chowder was sticking to it. The white wine was all right and he was going through it at a rate which was close to stretching the limits of politeness, but he'd have preferred large gins or vodkas.

"Very well, thanks," Rona answered. She went into some detail about the fashion scene and next season's lines.

"Anything for the thirty-something?" Julie inquired with a smile.

"Absolutely. Drop by some time and I'll give you the tour. And a good discount."

"That's a kind offer. I'll take you up on it. My wardrobe is getting a little tired."

Even when they started on the third bottle of wine the conversation remained awkward. Julie tried to lighten it – as if indeed she was a professional escort – but to little avail.

"I've been admiring that painting." Julie nodded towards a landscape that hung on the chimney piece directly in front of her. "There's a fresh summery feel to it."

"It was one of our favourite places." Niall said. "The southern end of Glacier Park. Look at the signature."

Julie crossed the room and bent to study it. "Your … daughter?"

"Yes. She could turn her hand to almost anything," Niall said. He remembered how the sun played on her features as she sketched the scene, sitting in a field of wild flowers that overlooked the glacial valley.

"I'm no expert. But she has … had a lot of talent." Julie sat down again. She couldn't win for losing. Her escort for the evening sat mute, unable or unwilling to come to her rescue. She never could figure out whether he was a cold fish or just socially inept.

The conversation meandered into politics, what was currently happening on the Hill. David permitted himself the observation that, after years of dancing around politicians on both sides of the Atlantic, he could not decide whether they were mad or bad.

"Mad as in sociopaths?" Niall queried.

"I don't think they're sociopaths," David said, "because that would mean they didn't really know the difference between good and evil. They do know the difference," he insisted. "They know what they're doing all right, but they don't care what harm they cause so long as it's not to themselves."

"I suppose," Niall offered, "they're like drug addicts. They may appear to be screwed up but they are fully aware of the damage they do to others."

David fell silent but Julie pronounced her agreement. "Drugs are no excuse for anything, and I'm not even sure that temporary insanity is a legitimate plea…" She decided not to elaborate because of other elephant traps that might be lying in wait. She knew nothing about these people, how they thought, acted, lived, but there was something about the way they interacted that was unsettling. It was not in any sense a pleasant or ordinary dinner party. There were moments when she'd have given her right arm to be able to walk away.

During coffee Niall left the table and returned with a photo album which he opened as soon as he sat down.

"You'll enjoy these, Julie." He slurred slightly. "Here's one of David which was taken when he came out here first. There he is standing by the moon buggy in the Air and Space Museum. A bit of a rube, eh?" He smiled as he pointed to the photo.

"You had a lot more hair back then." She turned to David, whose face was a mask.

"I'm not sure they're … interested," Rona began.

"Oh, of course we are," Julie rebutted gallantly. She put her left hand under the table and sneaked a look at her watch. This was worse than a visit to the dentist. She longed to be back in her apartment with her shoes off, sipping a Martini and watching a good movie on Netflix.

Niall pointed to a photo of Mark sitting on a sleigh with a little red ski cap on his head. He looked so innocent; all the friends and relations used to fawn over him.

"And who's that attractive little girl beside him?" Julie asked. But she realised with a pang who it was just before Niall answered.

"They were inseparable in those days. Whenever it snowed they'd head straight for the Marie Butler Levin Preserve. That's just on the other side of Kirby Road. It's got a great slope for sledding on. God, they used to have such fun..." Niall turned a page. "And there they are again, inseparable, playing T-ball. Look at the sweatshirts for Goodness sake. They were sponsored by the *Secretary's Friend*..."

"They're so cute..."

Niall nodded. There were tears in his eyes. The next picture showed the two kids playing on a swing set in the Highsmith's back yard near the pool.

"Ros always loved going over there," Niall said. "They used to make their own lemonade. Awful stuff as I recall but we all had to drink it. You remember that, David?"

"Yes ... It seems a long time ago..." David

felt pinpricks of sweat on his forehead and beneath his eyes. There was no wine left in any of the bottles on the table. He could have killed for a real drink; his own supply was literally across the street but there was no way he could get to it.

"Not to me," Niall said. "Not long at all. It could have been yesterday."

"How about a brandy?" Rona inquired by rote.

David nodded but Julie made a point of looking at her watch. "The time's just flown."

"It's only ten-fifteen," Niall said. He closed the album slowly and let his hand rest on the cover.

"I have a very busy day tomorrow. I need my beauty sleep." She thanked them for a most pleasant evening and hoped she would see them again soon. After a brief visit to the bathroom she re-joined David near the door where they made their farewells.

While they walked the hundred odd yards to David's house she held her peace, but once inside she rounded on him.

"Don't ever involve me in anything like that again." Angrily she removed her earrings and threw them in her purse.

"Like what?" He knew it had been awkward and he should have explained the situation to her in advance. But how could he have known that Niall would behave like that? Anyway Julie was overreacting. After all she wasn't on the hazard.

He poured himself a large vodka and downed half of it in one gulp.

"I don't know what was going on back there but I want none of it. I'm not some kind of fucking guinea-pig."

"They're just confused," he said. "Maybe still in shock or … what do you call it? … post-traumatic something-or-other?"

She gave him a withering look. "Just call me a cab."

"Stay the night, Julie." He tried to put his arm around her.

She offered him the palms of her hands. "Absolutely not. I may not have very high principles. But there are limits. Now please call me a cab."

"I'll drive you…"

"Christ, you drank about two bottles of wine back there and you've started again…" She let it go; his habits, however dangerous, were no concern of hers. "A cab will be fine."

He went to make the call, resigned to the fact that there would be no sex. But at least the goddamn dinner was over. When he hung up the receiver he fished in his wallet and handed her ten fifty-dollar bills. There was no attempt at delicacy on either side.

As she stacked the dishes in the washer, Rona's

silence smouldered and caught fire.

"What in god's name was that all about? The play's the thing wherein you'll catch the conscience of the king? You couldn't even look at those photos on your own. Yet you could produce them in front of … those people."

"I hated myself for doing it…but it had to be done…"

"I think you need help. You should see someone."

"David said the same about you." He was stung by her words. Maybe he had overdone it; he would have to learn.

"When did he say that? I didn't hear…"

"No, it was weeks ago, when I told him you'd hired an investigator…"

"You told him that?" She slammed the door of the dishwasher shut and confronted him. "Christ, you shouldn't have done that. No wonder he gave Diane a hard time…" Words failed her.

"We're never going to have enough evidence," he pointed out. "Not enough for an indictment. Anyway, David isn't the guilty party."

"My god, he's an accomplice after the fact. At the very least. You shouldn't car-pool with him anymore. Break off all contact, if you want my opinion … I nearly got sick watching him tonight in our house. It was a disaster … And that woman … Who is she?"

Niall suspected she was the woman he used

to see at lunchtime but he kept his own counsel. He had rarely seen Rona so upset and he didn't know what to say to her. It was as if she wanted to hit out in all directions and not just at the main culprit. He could identify with that feeling.

"I'm sorry…" was all he could say. He was apologising not only for the dinner party, if that's what it was, but also for being unable to help.

"Don't be sorry for me," she replied. "I'm trying to get on with my life. Maybe you should try it too."

What life, he wondered. After he put out the trash he went to bed feeling miserable. Rona joined him later and they lay there, back to back, each wondering if the other was asleep but too wary to ask.

CHAPTER 14

"YEAH, VAN GOGH wasn't the worst," Si conceded, "Though he didn't have both oars in the water. Poor bastard never sold a painting in his life. Now they're going for a hundred million apiece."

"I didn't know you studied art history," David said. It was a Friday and earlier that afternoon the ambassador had asked him if he could spend part of the weekend looking after a Minister who was due to visit Washington. David said he would have to check his calendar but he had used the excuse of domestic commitments so often in the past that it was wearing very thin. He put through a call to Whitehall and discovered that the Minister was a keen golfer. Since one of the First Secretaries at the Washington embassy was a scratch player he was the obvious choice and so David managed to pass the buck. It was a modest enough coup but he enjoyed it; minute victories like that had helped him maintain a semblance of sanity over the years.

"There was a very interesting write-up of Van Gogh in the recent issue of *The Washingtonian*," Niall said. "And apparently the Museum of Modern Art is mounting a big exhibition. I thought I'd look in on it." He sat in the back of the car, his briefcase on his lap.

"That museum you mentioned," Si began,

"that's the one they call MoMA, right? It's in New York." He pulled into a filling station and told the attendant to give him fifty bucks worth.

"Yes, it's in New York. That gives me an idea," Niall said. "I'd be happy to look in on Mark…"

"Oh, there's no need for that," David said. "He's getting on fine. Besides, why tear yourself away from the exhibition…?"

"Yeah," Si said. "You'll be rubbing shoulders with all those arty-crafty pseuds, having a wonderful time." Before paying for the gas he insisted on having the windscreen washed and the oil checked.

"It won't be a problem," Niall insisted. "I'll be glad to do it."

"Well … it might be awkward … He's shacked up, you know…"

"I'm a man of the world," Niall said lightly. "That doesn't bother me in the least. I could call at the restaurant first. It's that Italian place on Mott Street isn't it?"

"How did you know that?" David shifted uncomfortably in the passenger seat. The memory of that ghastly dinner party was still searingly fresh.

"You told me. Don't you remember? In fact, I could bring him and his girlfriend out for lunch."

"Good old Uncle Niall." Si checked the windscreen, pronounced it satisfactory and edged the car out into the traffic.

"I think he works the lunch shift," David said. This wasn't true but he could feign ignorance later if he had to. His eyes felt hot and grainy and he blinked frequently as if to massage the pupils with his eyelids.

"Have you guys not worked it out yet?" Si asked. "You couldn't organise a piss-up in a brewery. Take the kids out for dinner. Give 'em a slap-up meal. Youngsters need a lot of protein."

"Good idea." Niall turned to David, "You'd better give me the address of his apartment just to be on the safe side."

With some hesitation David rummaged in his wallet and produced the address. In normal circumstances he would have been ashamed to let anyone see that awful kip occupied by his son but that was now the least of his worries. He tried to console himself with the thought that if Mark was still in that amnesiac state there would be little cause for concern.

"That's settled then," Niall said. "It'll be just like old times."

"Well, if you're sure. It's very kind of you…"

"He's going to do it. My god we have a decision. At long last." Si had to stop behind a school bus which was letting off some of its passengers. It was against the law to overtake in such circumstances and it was a law which had always appealed to Niall. America could be rough and tough in many respects but it valued children, or so it had seemed to him.

"Is there any message you'd like me to give Mark?"

"Oh, just to take care of himself. And you might subtly suggest that he find a better apartment." David turned around and made eye contact. "Actually, between ourselves, I'm not sure his girlfriend – Sue is her name – is a good influence on him. I think she's heavily into drugs whereas he's working his programme." He sighed and made an appeal with his hands. "But you know kids. If you try to split them up it probably makes matters worse." He would of course have to warn Mark about the impending visit, which he would describe as a fishing expedition. He would advise him to go to a public place, if at all possible, and to bring Sue along.

They negotiated a bend in Kirby Road where years ago Niall had happened across Ros and Mark doing wheelies on their BMX bikes. He had spoken sternly to them about the dangers of cars coming suddenly around the corner. Even though his rebuke was directed mainly at Ros, who was something of a daredevil at that age, Mark had tried to put all the blame on her. Now as he looked at the back of David's head he felt queasy. It was no surprise that in the months since the tragedy, David had never made one reference to Ros. It was as if she never existed. Other friends and neighbours had been reluctant too, but gradually they took their courage in their hands and did their best to explain how her brief life had touched them. Not this cold son of a bitch who posed as a civilised man – and certainly not his ill-begotten spawn.

"I'm so glad that's settled," Si said. "You'd be lost in my kind of work, I can tell you. I have to make decisions on the hoof every day. Big decisions." He clicked his fingers in quick succession.

"Like what?" David asked.

"Like today I had to fire the new chef. It turned out that he likes women as much as they like his pastries. He was mashing the fat every day in the kitchen. He was even caught having a knee-trembler in the cold room. Amazing." He shook his head at the wonder of it all and the trials he had to bear. "Very talented people are nearly always prima donnas," he concluded.

If he was right, Niall thought, Ros was the exception.

One of his few remaining pleasures, as David himself termed it, was a lie-in on Saturday mornings. The anatomy of this pleasure was as follows: First, on waking there would be the slow realisation that there was no need to get up. This was occasionally enhanced by thinking it might still only be Friday and then becoming aware of the splendid error. Second, he would lie on his back to savour the awareness. (If he turned on his side he might fall asleep too quickly.) Third, to make sure he didn't fall asleep even on his back, he would reach out a lazy arm and turn the sound system on. Thus he would linger and bask in Schubert and it made no difference if he did doze off later on. Everything was permissible, one's mind reasonably blank, old fatigues and alcoholic toxins seeping out of muscles and stiffening joints, and for once there was no equating sleep with death.

This Saturday morning was different, however. The phone rang and he decided to answer it since his reverie was irretrievably broken. He didn't at first recognise the voice but then the penny dropped. Geoff, his friend at the UN who, after some phatic conversation, said, "I'm going to put Michael Cremin on. He's the doctor who called on Mark a couple of times as we agreed. He's the best there is."

"Thanks, Geoff. I appreciate it." David was now instantly awake.

Dr. Cremin introduced himself and entered the usual caveats about arm's-length diagnosis. In his view Mark had a serious drug problem but was not suffering from amnesia or any related pathology.

"But could a drug episode have the effect of a blackout?" David inquired

"Not really. The effect is quite different to that caused by alcohol abuse…"

"How about a … psychological thing? You

know, where one can block out a traumatic event…"

"That's possible," Cremin conceded. "But could you be more specific?"

"The accidental death of a close friend. Mark doesn't seem to accept that she's dead." David knew he was on safe ground with this version; anyway Cremin was well outside the loop.

"And he never accepted it?"

"He did at first." David recalled the funeral and the row they'd had. "But later on he seemed to go completely blank."

"That would be most unusual," Cremin said. "I haven't come across that in clinical work or in the journals…"

"But it's possible?"

Cremin uttered a short laugh. "There's so much we still don't understand. In a sense everything is possible. There could have been a delayed trigger that kicked in after the fact, as it were. It would be most unlikely but it can't be ruled out. I would have to do a lot more work with Mark to come to a definite opinion…"

David said he would have to think about that and discuss it with Mark. He reminded the doctor to send him his bill.

"Oh, I wouldn't hear of it," Cremin said. "We expats have to stick together."

David didn't quite know what to make of this assessment which was, as he should have expected, far from conclusive. He was relieved that there didn't appear to be a mental problem as such. On the other hand, hearing a doctor describe the addiction as serious was somehow more worrying than his own grasp of that reality. The question that had haunted him – and on which he was no wiser – was whether Mark was lying or whether he was really in denial. When he was young his deceptions had usually been fairly flimsy and obvious. Had he finally mastered the art and if so, to what purpose?

David looked at the alarm clock on his bedside table. It was eight-thirty. He couldn't go back to bed again. What on earth was he going to do with the rest of the day?

CHAPTER 15

ACROSS THE STREET Niall was also up early though to more purpose. He buttered two slices of toast, cut them into fingers and put them on a plate. He put the plate, a cup of coffee and a glass of orange juice on a tray and brought it upstairs to Rona, who was still in bed.

"It's not my birthday is it?" she asked, propping herself up on a pillow.

"It doesn't have to be…"

"No. I'm kidding. This is nice, Niall. Thanks." She surveyed him briefly and saw that he was more formally dressed than usual for a Saturday morning.

"What's up?"

"I'm going to New York."

"Why…? To see Mark? That's not a good idea, Niall. It'll muddy the water…"

"It was muddy from the very beginning … still is."

"It's a mistake. No useful purpose will be served. Keep away from him and his father. In fact, I don't know how you can tolerate being with them…"

"I don't think you trust my judgement very much, Rona. That's OK. I don't mind. But I'm learning…"

"I meant we should leave it to … the authorities." In a way he had read her right. She never saw him as a practical person, still less as a man of action.

"What authorities? What have they done to date? Nothing. And every day that passes the trail goes colder. You heard what Diane said … And you were right to hire her by the way … Why? Because the *authorities* can't hack it …If we were big contributors to political parties it might be different … but we're not. So that's it."

"I've got an appointment to see the Assistant DA in two weeks' time," Rona said.

"Two weeks," Niall repeated. "I rest my case. You know and I know how the political process works. This case isn't high-profile enough for them. We've no clout. There's no race angle involved. It has nothing to do with organised crime. It's just an ordinary, everyday murder. The DA's office wouldn't get any mileage out of it. Jesus Christ … They've hung us out to dry."

Rona looked at him as if seeing him for the first time. From the bedroom window she watched him get into the car and throw a suitcase onto the back seat. She thought long and hard about what might have been going on in his mind and why he was bringing a suitcase. She had no answers.

He drove into the short-term carpark of Reagan Airport and walked from there to the Eastern terminal. About ten minutes later he boarded the shuttle, paid for his ticket with Amex, declined a fruit juice and gazed out the window for most of the hour-long flight until the Manhattan skyline came into view.

At La Guardia he phoned the Italian restaurant on Mott Street and discovered that Mark would not be coming on duty until eight o'clock that evening. So David had lied; that came as no surprise. Because his stomach was unsettled he went to the bathroom and locked himself in a stall for a few minutes. Crouched and clutching his midriff, he recalled the self-same posture and sense of the unknown that he had experienced all those years ago on the night before he left the seminary for good. When he emerged from the stall he splashed water on his face and combed his thinning hair.

He decided to go straight to the apartment. As usual, it was far more difficult to get a cab than a plane. He stood patiently in line listening to the raucous exchanges between the drivers and dispatchers. It was a sellers' market; the would-be customers didn't count for anything and could be treated with contempt. If that particular line of people were to disappear another one would quickly form.

When he eventually got a cab it took a considerable amount of time to explain to the driver the exact location of the address and even then Niall had to suggest several course corrections during the journey. Most of these did not appear to be comprehensible to the driver who had little English. Niall gave up and when they got close to Chinatown he paid the fare, got out and walked. It was a market area with an overpowering smell of fish. He asked a couple of stall-owners for directions but to no avail. One Chinese woman obviously thought he wanted to buy something and she held up several unrecognisable and disgusting crustaceans for his inspection.

He knew he must have appeared conspicuous, especially with a suitcase in his hand, and though he didn't feel in danger, he thought it might just press his luck to consult the map he had downloaded, in the middle of the street. He went into a tea house and ordered a glass of rice wine. He placed the map on the table, put on his reading glasses and, after several minutes of intense scrutiny, found his bearings. He re-folded the map, paid for the wine and left.

He had little difficulty in finding the rooming house, which was a derelict building propped on both sides by timber baulks, its front façade defaced by a rusting fire escape. He mounted the front steps, pushed open the graffiti-daubed door and found himself in a dismal lobby. A hatch flew open in the wall to his left. Through the gloom he could barely make out the face of an unshaven man who asked him what his business was. Niall said he wanted to call on Mark Highsmith, one of the tenants. The name didn't mean anything to the super, who asked for a description instead. Niall supplied one as best he could, adding that there was a girl staying with him as well.

"The British hophead moved in with *her*," The Super corrected him. He eyed the suitcase suspiciously then jerked his thumb towards the stairs. "Top of the house," he said.

Niall climbed the stairs, which reeked of stale urine and some exotic spice which he couldn't identify. Judging by the sounds he heard on the lower landings it was apparent that several young families lived in this rat-hole. He had not seen such an appalling slum since the late sixties when the Master of Studies in Maynooth had brought the class to visit a tenement in the poorest part of Dublin. As far as he knew, most of the slums of European cities had long since been demolished and replaced by clean, though modest, accommodations. It was difficult to understand why this had not happened in the richest and most powerful country in the world. It occurred to him that the people living in this squalid and dangerous building probably felt lucky to have a home at all.

When he got to the top floor he paused for breath, then rang the bell of the apartment door. A trickle of sweat ran between his shoulder blades as he became conscious of a presence on the other side of the door. He felt sure that someone was appraising him through the peep-hole. The door opened a few inches to reveal a girl's waif-like face tilted to one side.

"You must be Sue," he said quickly. "I'm

Niall Grenham, a friend of Mark's."

"Just a second." She disappeared and he could hear her repeating his name in a tense whisper. Through a chink in the door he could see a figure in boxer shorts drag himself out of bed and then, suddenly, the familiar face stared out at him, blinking against the light.

"Hi, Mark, I'm visiting New York and I told your Dad I'd drop by."

Mark slowly removed the chains from the door and let him in. "It's good to see you … but I have to get to work soon."

"It's only eleven-thirty. Relax. Give yourself a chance to wake up." Niall extended his hand to Sue. "I'm glad to meet you."

"Yeah … same here … Would you like a cup of coffee?"

"I could kill for one, thanks," Niall said with a smile. Turning to Mark he added, "Sorry to barge in on you like this. I thought David might have told you…"

"No," Mark said abruptly. "No, he said nothing. I haven't heard from him." He passed a hand through his hair in a futile attempt to tidy it. Then he pulled on a pair of pants and a denim shirt. After that his hands still seemed restless.

Niall was pretty sure that David had warned his son, but he didn't pursue the matter. "Well, I think he was keen for me to stop by since he hasn't had the chance to visit recently." The air-conditioning unit on the window coughed and died. Sue hit it with the heel of her hand and got it going again.

"Right," Mark agreed.

"But he was here a few days ago." Sue turned from the gas ring to face them. She fluffed up a rather lank and skimpy ponytail with a distracted hand.

"That was Uncle Toby," Mark said. With a grin he added, "Sue hasn't figured out the family yet."

"I know the feeling." Niall noticed how Mark's forehead lifted when he lied, as if he were trying to widen his eyes. He had done it even as a kid. The movement had the effect of shifting the scalp over the cranium. "Thanks," he said as Sue handed him a coffee. He placed it on top of a bedside locker made from cheap plywood – one that had obviously come in a flat pack. In a way he felt sorry for Sue even though he knew that she had informed on Mark. How could a young woman live in such squalor? The strange thing was – and it came as a shock to him – that he almost felt sorry for Mark too. It was ridiculous.

"Everything OK at work?" Niall inquired.

"Not too bad. It's just a temporary job of course."

"What would you like to do eventually?"

Mark thought for a while. "Acting." He went by the script. "Or directing."

Sue gave him a surprised glance; it was obviously news to her and she was beginning to enjoy the intrigue.

"Tough business," Niall said. "Especially in this town. Or so I'm told. Have you had any auditions yet?"

"No, not yet. I'm still pounding the pavements."

"I'd find auditions very difficult," Niall said. "Having to perform to order. And then being rejected. It must be humiliating."

"Yes, it must be awful," Sue said with a measure of sarcastic overstatement. She sat cross-legged on the bed, holding her coffee cup with both hands.

"Are you in town on business?" Mark asked hurriedly, to prevent her from making some other disparaging comment.

"No. I want to see the Van Gogh exhibition at MoMA."

"I wouldn't mind seeing it myself."

"Why not come with me? Both of you. My treat." In other circumstances Niall could have been an uncle calling on a couple of students in a fraternity house to invite them out for a square meal and a show. He had to remind himself that one was a murderer and both were drug addicts.

"Thanks all the same," Mark said. "But the job, such as it is, comes first. Maybe a rain-check?" The thought of spending half a day in an art gallery with this boring old fart was almost amusing.

"Fine." Niall opened the suitcase, took out a landscape painting and handed it to Mark. "Do you recognise the scene?"

Mark studied it and shook his head slowly. "It looks vaguely familiar but I can't place it."

"The Shenandoahs. Remember, we all went there for your tenth birthday. Ros painted it afterwards, largely from memory. Anyway I want you to have it as a memento…"

"I couldn't…"

"Go on, take it. She'd want you to have it." He laid it on the bed. "I'm going to leave it there for you."

"Thanks."

"Who exactly is Ros?" Sue had of course heard the name but never managed to fit it into the scheme of things. As far as she could recall – it was all a bit fuzzy – the PI hadn't said much about her.

"My daughter," Niall said. "She and Mark went to the same school. They grew up together. They were inseparable." He patted her arm. "It was all platonic of course."

"Then why … I mean, you mentioned something about a memento." Sue nodded towards the painting.

"Oh, you didn't know?" Niall faltered, full of self-loathing, then continued with an effort. "She died in a tragic … accident."

"I'm … sorry." Sue began to put it together; it was all becoming clearer now. And she had an instinct that there could be something here which, with a little manipulation, could be turned to good advantage.

"I want you to have this as well." Niall

brought out a tennis trophy – two gilt figurines on top of a mahogany plinth. He pressed it into Mark's hands. "Mixed doubles, St. John's Juniors, 1979. Look at the inscription … Both your names. Do you remember the presentation ceremony?"

"I … remember."

"We have to concentrate on the good times," Niall said. "That's all we can do. And try to rebuild our lives. There's a lot more stuff in the case which I'll leave with you. There's even a lock of her hair…" He had debated long and hard with himself about that particular item and his decision to give it to Mark did not come easy. "You can go through it with Sue. It's important to remember the past, at least not to block it out."

"Thank you … I don't know what to say."

"You don't have to say anything. It's OK … Well…" Niall placed his hands on his knees and stood up. "I'll get out of your hair. And I apologise, Sue, for barging in like this."

"Not at all, Mr. Grenham … It was nice to meet you."

"Incidentally, I hope you won't be offended but I'd like you to have a good night out on me. I know how tough it is for young people starting out in the city." He produced an envelope of cash from an inside pocket and ignored some faint murmurs of protest. He stuck the envelope in the pocket of Mark's shirt.

"Oh, there's really no need."

"Not at all. It's nothing. Will you walk with

me to the stairs?"

Mark followed him out into the foetid corridor. When they reached the top landing Niall said, "I didn't want to upset Sue but there's something I should tell you because you'll probably hear about it sooner or later. The police have finally come to the view that Ros's death was not an accident."

"Oh my god." The blood drained from Mark's face. That black bitch was bad enough. But the police … since when had they become involved?

"They're now convinced it was murder. Hard to believe? I know. That was my reaction too."

"Are you sure? I mean…"

"There are a lot of very sick people out there. Call me any time, Mark. If there are any more souvenirs you want just let me know." They shook hands and Niall started down the stairs. His legs felt weak.

Back in the room Sue was on her knees going through the suitcase. "What the hell was all that weird shit about?"

"Who knows?" Mark feigned indifference though he was badly shaken. His father would do anything to prevent a scandal but he wasn't all-powerful.

"He's crazy…" From the case she took out a card written in a childish hand inviting Mark to a slumber party. "How sweet. Even a lock of hair, for fuck's sake." She emptied the contents on to the bed and sorted through them. "All this crap and five cents wouldn't buy you a cup of coffee." Becoming conscious of his silence, she threw him a glance. "What's the matter with you?"

"Nothing." He clawed at the soft tissue of his neck just beneath the chin.

A thought occurred to her. "Hey, give me a look at that envelope."

Absent-mindedly, Mark took it from his pocket and handed it to her.

"Jesus Christ!" She examined the contents carefully. "Holy shit … it's five grand…"

"It couldn't be."

She pulled him over to look at it. "He may be crazy but he must think a lot of you."

"I wonder…" A canny, reflective light came into his pale face. It was far too much but there was no mistake. He couldn't for the moment make any sense of it but that in itself put him on tilt.

"At least it's better than all this junk." She waved a disparaging arm over the memorabilia scattered on the counterpane of the bed. "A lot better." She fanned herself, holding the envelope by a corner. "This isn't chump change. This is real spending money. You just hang in there. I'll be back in a half hour. We'll be fine, baby." And there was more where that came from if she played her cards right. Uncle Niall wasn't that hard to see through.

Because he had some time to kill, Niall did in fact go to see the Van Gogh exhibition but, despite the magnetic pull of those powerful canvases, his mind was elsewhere. The tour guide showed them the latest acquisition, *Irises*, which had been bought a few years previously by MoMA for the paltry sum of eighty million bucks. And the artist couldn't even afford to buy paint during his life and died a pauper. That was all Niall could focus on; the injustice and crushing obscenity.

In the art shop he bought a print and a hand-painted stone for Rona and then emerged into the muggy heat of Manhattan. Despite the hugeness of the city he always felt it lacked substance. It was more like the studio lot of some epic movie: all front. He wandered around for a while breathing in that peculiar mixture of smells that contained food spices, diesel fumes, vented steam and sewage. The homeless were everywhere with their little trolleys and grocery carts of belongings. He recalled one of Si's less funny observations, "They're lucky; no overheads."

At that time of day it wasn't too difficult to get a cab and he was on the shuttle by five o'clock. It brought him up short when he realised he didn't want to get home too early. It never used to be like that. In fact the opposite was the case – when he had a complete family. His heart went out to Rona. Had she sensed this change in him?

When he got out of the terminal in Reagan his movements were slow, lethargic as if he were still walking in the melted tar of New York. What had he accomplished? Probably nothing. But if he stopped, he knew he would never be able to start again.

At home he deduced from his voicemail that Rona had probably gone out with Betty. The house was so empty he could hardly bear it and he longed for his wife to come home. The sitting room was lit by the eerie blue light of the TV, which was silent for the most part though it gave an occasional crackle. When Rona did return, at about eleven p.m., she hardly acknowledged his presence and made no reference to his ill-conceived trip. Her silence was wounding.

The following morning, after the graveyard shift, Mark and Sue lay together as high as kites. The hypo, collar and cotton as well as the large stash of heroin, could be seen in a tin box that protruded from beneath the bed.

"Jesus … that was some dog food," Sue moaned. "…no end to … the rush. It just keeps on … happening…" Her face was a mask of pleasure. "Don't nod out, man…" She caressed his neck and the back of his head.

"Good old … Uncle Niall." Mark made an effort to keep his eyes open. To sleep away the effects of a hundred dollar hit would be a waste. Besides, when she came down a bit she would want sex. He liked it when she took the lead.

"And I figured it … all out … the whole ball of wax…" It was time to play a good card though she would keep the ace for the time being.

"Good for you…" He laughed with her. Even if the cops had started an investigation how far would they get? Dumb bastards, all of them.

"You're crazier than me … You know that? And you kept … quiet about it all this time…"

"I'm a quiet kind of guy." His rush had now changed to a more subtle sensation of floating. It was glorious and would last forever. The promise of rough sex was beginning to make itself felt in his loins.

"You did in Uncle Niall's little sweetie pie and never said a word. You took her out, and I don't mean on a date."

"A stuck up little bitch," Mark said. "And a tease."

"Did she upset my little mensch?" Sue ogled him with her index finger.

"Not for long," Mark said. They both laughed, then grew serious as Sue pushed him back on the bed and began to take her clothes off.

CHAPTER 16

AS SOON AS the gardener left, David got into his swimming trunks and dived into the pool. He re-surfaced, shaking his head vigorously and gradually developed a rhythm, breathing from both sides alternately. It was such relief; the water washing over him. Not like that night, the night of the alibi when he swam as if his life depended on it. Maybe it would all pass in time, just as the water flowed silkily over him. After a few lengths he got out of the pool to fetch a snorkel which allowed him to swim without raising his head. He wanted to stay under for as long as possible as if complete immersion could keep reality at bay.

But thoughts kept bubbling up to the surface. His most recent phone conversation with Mark had brought him back to square one. Mark had sounded edgy, as if he'd come down from a bad trip. He told him about Niall's visit and how weird it had been. They discussed the possibility of police involvement, with David tending to discount it as a bluff, though he couldn't be sure.

"Why did he give me all that stuff?" Mark had asked, as if a parent should know these things.

"I don't know," David replied. "But don't let it rattle you. He may genuinely want you to have those items."

"I have to look at the bloody things every

day…"

"Christ, throw them out then," David said in exasperation.

"What if he calls again?" This question did not evoke a response and after a while he added, "You shouldn't have sent that shrink."

"I was concerned…" David knew how hollow that must have sounded, and how precious. A long silence ensued after which Mark said in a diffident, almost pleading tone, "It was … an accident, you know…"

"For god's sake, last month you said you couldn't remember." There was even less reason to believe him now. Maybe the blackout ploy had been a subconscious attempt to put the clock back and thereby signified remorse but, try as he might, David could not quite bring himself to believe that. His son's erratic 'memory' could prove to be a serious liability. That was the thought he was left with when Mark ended the conversation by hanging up without warning.

After a long while, maybe twenty-five leisurely lengths, he became conscious of an unaccustomed shadow on the water. He raised his head to see Niall watching him, the light behind his back. He was dressed in beige slacks, polo shirt and sandals. How long had he been there?

"Hi, Niall," He removed the snorkel. "I didn't see you."

"I hope I'm not interrupting your routine."

"No. I've probably done more than is good

for me." He clambered out of the pool and draped a towel around his shoulders. They sat at a patio table and drank iced water.

"You used to swim, didn't you?"

"Yes," Niall said. "Not any more." His face was still in shadow.

"Why not?"

"I never really liked it." He didn't elaborate.

"It's good to have an Indian summer," David remarked. "as long as it's not a sign of global warming. Anyway, it'll shorten the winter."

Niall nodded. On that they could agree. There wasn't in fact much direct sunlight; the heat seemed to be reflected from some other source. He produced a birthday card from his pocket and laid it on the table. It showed a young girl on a skateboard; inside it read: 'To Ros, with every best wish on your tenth birthday, Love, Uncle David'.

"This would have been her twenty-second birthday," Niall said. "A short life … If things had been different she could be here with us right now … sitting at this table."

David bowed his head unable to say anything.

"She kept every card you ever sent her. You can have this one."

"Are … you sure…?"

"Yes."

David hesitated. "Mark really appreciated the things you gave him. But if you ever have a change of heart and want them back. Then of course…"

"No, no, that's all right." Niall looked at the sky which was virtually cloudless, an endless gunmetal space. "She was very fond of you and Mark."

"And we … of her," David said awkwardly. "One can't comprehend such a disaster … out of a clear blue sky…" He wanted to crumple the card and throw it away but instead he stared at it and ran his fingertips along the edges.

"It was no accident."

"Are you absolutely sure?" David's brow wore a furrowed look of concern.

"Murder, I'm afraid. We have the evidence now." A light breeze ruffled the surface of the pool. A cardinal bird broke cover from a beech tree, its sudden exit causing a few leaves to float down to the dry grass.

"Investigators sometimes…" David began slowly, "…may be inclined to exaggerate, so as to justify…"

"Not this one, and the police are in on it now. Besides, I've done a lot of research myself. *I know*."

"But who…?" David spread his hands in a gesture of helpless inquiry. "I mean, it's not as if Ros had any enemies."

He would talk about her now, Niall thought, because his back was against the wall. That was the only reason. Like father, like son. He hated the way he said her name; it was sacrilegious.

"She had one, apparently. A snake in the

grass … who waited, bided his time … and then when the opportunity came he followed her and drove her off the road."

"Premeditated?" David's voice was no more than a whisper as he squinted against the light.

"Oh yes. Carefully thought out." Niall watched as the other man put on a pair of sunglasses which he fished out of a pocket of his robe.

"What on earth could the motive have been?" Although David felt faint he was conscious of the thudding of his heart. The sunglasses didn't help; he felt trapped.

"Jealousy. She was on the threshold of a happy and successful life. He had blown away all his chances."

"Are you saying that … he knew her well?" David lowered his glance, focusing on the terracotta tiles that surrounded the pool. From two gardens over, came the high-pitched excited sounds of children at play.

"Yes."

"A friend of the family?"

"Yes."

"But who, Niall? We move in a fairly small circle. Do I know him?" He pulled the towel around his chest as if to conceal the heartbeats.

"Yes, you know him."

"My god … not that Brouwer kid?"

"No. There's no real harm in him." Niall let the silence develop as he gazed into the middle distance. "He would never hurt anyone, let alone kill them."

"I would respect a confidence, you know that. But if you'd rather not say, then I understand … especially as it could only be an opinion at this stage."

"Oh, it's more than that, believe me." Niall rotated the drinking glass between thumb and forefinger, leaving evanescent prints on the frosted surface.

"But you're not a lawyer, Niall. You're not au fait with the rules of evidence, any more than I am." David desperately hoped he would leave. He wasn't sure how much longer he could handle this without betraying himself by word or gesture.

"It's open and shut," Niall said. "The D.A. has the file. In his opinion it's only a question of time." This was pure fabrication but David was in no position to second guess him.

"I see." David's lips and throat were dry and there was a bottle of chilled vodka just ten feet away.

"A week at most." Niall glanced at his watch and got to his feet. "I've some calls to make." As he left the garden he thought that something had been achieved. The towel that David had draped himself in hadn't quite concealed the throbbing in his neck veins. He would also realise later the mistake he'd made. He should have asked if the killer was still at large in the neighbourhood. That missing inquiry spoke volumes and it would stab deep when it dawned on him. Constant, relentless pressure was required, then something would give. He wasn't sure what form it would take or what the precise mechanism would be but he would never let up. The fact that at times his behaviour disgusted him was of no account. He would never sit still or let the dust settle but would continue to seek out the pressure points.

He drove to the A&P grocery store to get some items for Rona. On the way home he stopped off to watch a Little League baseball game at the municipal park. He sat on the bleachers with other parents who urged on their kids. It was a mistake for him to go there, a bad mistake. He left quickly and sat in the car for a long time until he recovered enough to drive.

Late that evening, he had a call from David to say he was taking the next day off work and wouldn't be car-pooling. It was a matter-of-fact call but Niall regarded it as significant, though he couldn't say why. He decided to take the day off as well.

He stayed up late that night – long after Rona had gone to bed. In reviewing the options he considered it most likely that David would go to New York, father and son, colluding, comparing notes. If only he had the wherewithal to bug the apartment; it was a fanciful thought but he filed it away for future reference. As it turned out, his prediction about David's movements was wide of the mark.

The next morning he was up at six, not having slept very well. Between then and eight he sat on a chair placed in front of the bay window of the living-room which gave on to the house across the street. At a few minutes past eight he saw David get into the jeep and reverse it down the driveway. Niall rushed out, jumped into his own car and followed the jeep at a safe distance. By the time they reached Key Bridge he knew that David was not going to the airport. He was even more mystified when be realised that David was following his normal route to work. Niall parked about two hundred yards away and watched the jeep go through the barrier into the embassy carpark. He didn't know what to make of it – unless David had simply decided to opt out of the car pool, and of course he would have had good reason for such a decision. There was little point in waiting. At first Niall thought he might as well go to his own office but, on reflection, since he had already told Jack Wyndham he would be on a day's leave, he decided to go home. Rona would be at work, however, and the thought of wandering around the large empty house on his own did not greatly appeal to him. He wasn't interested in gardening any more or in keeping abreast of current affairs on the news channel. Some compromise was called for; he decided to call to one of the building sites on the way home.

Although the site manager showed him every courtesy and brought him into the prefab for a cup of coffee and a look at the plans, it became apparent to Niall that his presence there served no useful purpose. In fact he was probably getting in the way. He knew that Jack Wyndham had insisted on inserting a stiff penalty clause into the contract, so time meant money to this crew of subcontractors. After the second worker came into the cabin with a problem for the site manager, Niall knew it was time to go. Everything was working smoothly in any case.

It was about eleven when he got home and to his amazement he saw the jeep parked outside David's house. His first instinct was to hide his own car but he thought better of it. Why not let him see it and add confusion to confusion? He parked in full view and went indoors trying to figure it out. David had said he wasn't going to work but he did, and he stayed for what, no more than an hour at most. He didn't know what that signified but he felt an explanation would emerge sooner or later. Was the fissure beginning to show?

He was still puzzling over it when Rona came home with some take-away food which they picked at in silence. Eventually she said, "You didn't go to work today?"

"No."

"I suppose you were doing … your own thing." She pushed an uneaten hamburger away from her.

"What has to be done," he corrected mildly.

"That's your opinion." She flicked through the TV channels by rote. Impressed by none of them she switched off the set and threw the remote aside. They had always collaborated before, talked things out. Not only was his strange behaviour misguided in her opinion, he persisted in it without even referring to her, whereas once he would have pestered her for advice before coming to a decision on the smallest matter. They should have been pulling together, not going their separate ways. Pain was supposed to be a unifying force and if it didn't have that modest compensation then all was lost. She was glad she had arranged to meet Betty later that evening; it would be a relief to get out of the house, which was turning into a mausoleum.

Betty, who had sent her better half out bowling, to his grateful astonishment, listened carefully to Rona and then asked, "Why is Niall behaving like that? It doesn't sound like him. I suppose Ros's death unhinged him a little bit. I wouldn't worry though. He'll come round in the end."

"I wonder," Rona said. "He doesn't seem to believe in anything, least of all the legal system. I think some switch has been thrown. He wants to do it all himself. As if it's a duty or something…"

"Maybe revenge?" Betty didn't pull her punches.

Rona mulled over this for a while. A few months ago she'd have sworn that he didn't have a vengeful bone in his body, but now she wasn't so sure. Certainly his recent behaviour had something in it of righteous anger. Her restless fingers played with the beads of a necklace. It reminded her of how Niall used to say the rosary; oddly, she couldn't remember when he gave up the practice.

"He trained for the priesthood, didn't he?" Betty asked. Something of a coffee snob, she sipped her fresh brew of Jamaican Blue Mountain and made a mental note to add cinnamon in the future.

"That makes it even more difficult to understand."

"Whatever is going on in his mind, he's basically a good man. I have no doubt about that. None."

Rona didn't disagree. "I just don't know where he's coming from. He doesn't talk about it. The worst part is that he may well jeopardise everything."

"I don't follow."

"I can't say much about it yet. But all these hints and innuendoes … well, it's like serving notice. He's giving away the high ground."

"Try to talk to him," Betty advised. "In a calm way. Tell him you're confused and hurt and that you genuinely want to know what's going on. I know, I know… it sounds twee, agony aunt stuff. But you know what men are like. If you come on strong they feel threatened and clam up. You've got to give them a chance. They're not as tough as they make out."

Having reflected on this for a while, Rona

gave a wan smile. "You're not just a pretty face," she said.

"I'm not even a pretty face," Betty countered. She took no pride in the fact that her theory, which Si had debunked, had just been validated.

CHAPTER 17

A SIZEABLE CHEQUE from Niall had arrived in the post and though Mark had mixed feelings about it, especially after the earlier infusion of cash, he was in no position to look a gift horse in the mouth. This time he kept Sue in the dark and he used it for his own habit, which was imperceptibly growing out of control. His performance at work had deteriorated faster than his ability to cover up. He knew he was being watched by Francesco but it didn't bother him unduly.

The night after the wine cellar inventory was carried out provided the best opportunity for the staff to squirrel away a couple of bottles for themselves. Everyone knew it went on, including Francesco, and he didn't seem to mind as long as the pilfering wasn't overdone. Mark was so stoned, however, that he went for an entire case of Barolo which he secreted among the trash in the back alley, to be collected later.

"It's too much," the chef tried to warn him.

"No problemo," Mark said. "Don't worry about it." He floated from table to table, getting orders mixed up, making bizarre excuses and rude apologies. Even in the hectic atmosphere of the restaurant, where most of the clientele were probably on controlled substances of one kind or another, his behaviour attracted attention. In some recess of his mind he knew he was close to the edge but it didn't bother him. In fact he found it exhilarating. In a quiet moment Sue offered him a downer but he shrugged it aside with a laugh and a disproportionate flourish.

A little later, after he'd regaled a party of six with a blue joke, which in other circumstances they might have found amusing, the head waiter beckoned to him.

"I want to see you in the kitchen."

"I have to do table nine," Mark said. "They're ready for the old *gelato*."

"In the kitchen. Now."

The door was still swinging when Francesco rounded on him, "You dumb bastard. How many warnings do you need?"

"Chill out, man. Take it easy." Mark was too mellow to care.

"Did you think you were going to get away with it? The wine, all those fuck-ups, insulting the clients…"

"Aw, Cookie, you told him about the wine. That was our little secret."

"You're zonked, pal," Francesco spat out. "You're also fired. Take off that suit and get the fuck out of here. We're trying to run a business."

"Fine," Mark said. "I'll miss you spag-benders and all your little ways…"

The head waiter was about to take a swing at him but Francesco restrained him. Before Mark left he caught sight of Sue and blew her a kiss.

He wandered around the streets for a while and as he began to come down he was dimly aware of having passed another point of no return. Afraid to let the realisation penetrate too deeply, he looked for his contact. He needed another score, just one more. He waited in a shadowy arcade where the shop fronts were protected by steel shutters padlocked to bolts set into the concrete paving. After a while a dealer, not the usual one, materialised behind him. The transaction was quickly accomplished – a five-spoon bag for three hundred dollars and a couple of speedballs for another fifty. He felt the reassuring bulk of the stash in his inside pocket as he hastened back to the apartment with the same sense of euphoric anticipation as when, in his early teens, he rushed home with a pornographic magazine tucked in his armpit.

He imagined locking the door from the inside, getting the equipment from the box under the bed, roping a vein and then lying back as the H kicked in and the cracks in the ceiling smiled down on him. But he was coming down fast and still had four blocks to go. Heedlessly, he popped the speedballs and felt the effects almost immediately. It was better than he'd experienced before. The relaxation was so sudden and absolute that he felt as if he were falling, but this was accompanied by a profound feeling of empowerment. There was nothing he couldn't do. He knew he was stoned but it was of no consequence because nothing could hurt him, even the brightly-lit traffic that streamed in his direction.

He never made it to the apartment. Some twenty minutes later he was picked up by the police as he staggered down the centre of Delancy Street. He offered no resistance even when the handcuffs went on or when he was shoved into a holding tank with other felons of the night. It was another experience to be savoured in the course of his intense, once-in-a-lifetime trip.

———————

When Si returned to the table with the drinks he commented on the tea.

"I've been drinking too much coffee," Niall explained. In fact his stomach had been acting up for some time.

Si sat down beside him and sipped his beer, looking out at the eighteenth green clearly visible through the glass-walled lounge. Both men had come to the club house to pick up their wives, who were playing a round of golf. They had planned to have lunch together.

Si consulted his watch. "I thought they'd be coming up the eighteenth fairway by now. There's no sign of them. Women golfers. They've stopped for a chat somewhere." He looked down at the four-ball that was just finishing up. "That must've been some needle match," he said.

"How can you tell?" Niall never fully

understood the intricacies of the game and its protocols.

"That guy in the blue shirt made Marty putt out. And by any standards it was a gimme. Poor form if you ask me. Incidentally, why didn't you play today?"

"Lack of willpower. I opted for a Saturday morning lie-in." That was only partly true. He had less time than ever for that ridiculous game that turned so many men into fanatics and pseudo-experts.

"I was up at cockcrow," Si said in a complaining tone that had something of boastfulness in it too. "I have to get the books in order for a damn audit. Those IRS numb-nuts don't give you a chance. It's a wonder we have any entrepreneurs left in this country." He continued at some length about the burden of taxation and how the private sector was being stifled and hounded by Big Government. The Washington swamp still hadn't been drained and he doubted if it ever would be. Shading his eyes against the verdant flare, he peered through the window to see a three-ball come round the beech trees that formed the dogleg on the last fairway. "Still no sign of them. They went out at tennish. It's now almost two. They've been out for four hours already. Then they'll take ages in the locker room. I'm famished. The hell with it, I'm not going to wait any longer." He ordered a club sandwich and looked to Niall who said he wasn't hungry.

"And another thing," Si continued, "what's with you and David these days?"

"How do you mean?"

"The car pool for instance. You could cut the atmosphere with a knife … all those awkward silences. And you've both cried off the Neighbourhood Watch. I have to do it on my own. What's going on?" Si wore, what was for him, an unusually serious expression.

"I think … you must be imagining things."

"It's not just me," Si responded with some irritation and gestured around the club-room. "Ask anyone else here or in McLean. We're not all imagining things." He fell on the sandwich which had just appeared at his elbow, then opened it for inspection and applied a little more mustard.

"I didn't realise…" Niall began. "There is something. But I can't say too much at the moment."

"Some kind of feud?" Si pressed between mouthfuls.

"In a way, I suppose … I'm sorry."

Si studied him closely then his eyes widened suddenly. "Oh Christ, is it to do with the accident?" He suddenly recalled his conversation with Betty that Saturday in the garden, and knew that she was right. "I'm sorry I brought it up. Look, I wasn't being curious. It's just, well, more like concern."

"I know," Niall said. He began to realise that the time for direct confrontation had come. His first instinct was to get to it immediately but then he thought of David's habit of drinking on his own in the evening, especially on weekends. If he was running true to form he would be well liquored up by about eleven that night. That would be the best time to approach him.

Si announced that the errant spouses could at last be seen coming up the fairway, deep in conversation. Rather guiltily, he brushed crumbs off his sweater and put the empty plate on a nearly table. He might have to eat another sandwich for appearances' sake when they arrived.

At about ten-thirty that night Niall said he would take the dog for a walk. Rona expressed surprise, given the lateness of the hour, but didn't make an issue of it. She had planned to sit down with him the next day, after Sunday lunch, and have a frank discussion about their differing reactions. That had been the burden of the advice she received from Betty and some of the members of her group – and it made a lot of sense.

Niall left the wicket gate open so that Hamm could find his own way back to the kennel in the garden. He took the leash off and crossed the road. The upper part of David's house was in darkness but there was a telltale light in one of the downstairs windows. On opening the door, David gave him an excessively hearty greeting and led him down a short flight of steps into the den which doubled as a study and housed his books, drinks cabinet and sound system.

"Welcome to the bunker," David said. "Join me?"

Niall accepted a scotch and almost filled the glass with water and ice cubes.

"Cheers," he said with as much bonhomie as he could manage. The den really did look like a bunker and smelled of damp. It must have been off-limits to the cleaning lady and to most visitors.

David sank heavily into a well-worn recliner, where he was surrounded by the yellow-orange light of a standard lamp. He drained his own glass and re-filled it. "I guess I need this stuff." He drank liberally.

"Well, at least you can control it," Niall said. "Some people are not so lucky."

"And by 'some people' you mean?"

"Well, I suppose Mark for one. He's not so lucky…"

"Yeah. The apple doesn't fall far from the tree." David raised the footrest of the recliner and one of his tartan carpet slippers fell off. He didn't bother to retrieve it.

"I'm not with you." For some reason Niall's attention was distracted by the sight of the fallen slipper,

"Oh, I suppose Mark gets his, what-you-call-it, double helix from me … Addictive propensity and all that. Latest news bulletin: he was picked up by the police high as a kite in the Big Apple. Lost his job too, such as it was."

"I'm sorry to hear that." Niall brought the glass to his lips and pretended to drink.

"I don't know where he gets the cash from. Hope he's not into crime."

"Crime?"

"Stealing, shoplifting, that sort of thing."

"I see." Niall had to fight for control. Did this drunken moron not realise what his evil spawn had already done? Of course he did.

"No real harm in him though," David continued. "Just a dodgy gene somewhere." He peered at the lustrous amber in his glass. "Poison, you know, this stuff, medically speaking … a poison that you need … Oxymoron eh?"

"Mark will be OK," Niall said with an effort. "He's just a late developer."

David looked blearily at him. "My fault, I suppose. Have to be demonstrative nowadays, especially with Millennials … How does that bumper sticker go? Have you hugged your kid today? Jesus, it's such a crock. We're supposed to know what's going on inside." He hammered a forefinger against his chest.

"And what is going on inside?" Niall asked carefully, still testing the water. He re-filled David's glass.

"Mark? Who knows?"

"You."

"Nothing now … Maybe once but I've forgotten. Flushed it all out with scotch and vodka." His laughter rang false.

Niall didn't want to waltz around anymore. Maybe there would be a better opportunity in the future but he wasn't prepared to wait. The moment had come. He paused for breath, then leant forward. "You know, don't you?" He spoke quietly, almost soothingly.

"What?" David laid aside his glass. "What do I know?"

"The time for fencing is over." Niall was sick of it all, sick of his own part in it. In a way he was pleading for the final admission that would free them both.

"You're the one who's been doing that." David seemed to sober up. A haunted look passed over his face, reflecting a knowledge that Niall, though weak in many ways, would never give up or deviate from his present path.

"Yes. But it's time now for the truth." His body tensed up, almost went into spasm. "It's time."

"Maybe it is … maybe it isn't."

"So you're aware of what I know?" Niall asked breathlessly. He heard the ice cubes rattle in his glass. Say it, he thought. Say it, damn you.

"I'm aware of what … you think you know."

"Are you denying it?"

"Does it matter what I say or don't say?"

"Yes, it matters. It matters a great deal. To me and to you as well. Imagine the relief of getting rid of that awful burden of guilt." Say it. For Christ's sake, say it. His vision began to blur; he felt as if he were about to pass out.

"Are you accusing me?" David didn't look at him but kept his eyes fixed on a spot beneath a Dalí print on the opposite wall.

"Not you … Mark. But if you admit it, he will too." Niall held the cool glass against his throbbing forehead but it gave little relief.

"Suppose he's not aware of anything?"

"How could…?"

"Blackout."

"No." It was a partial admission, Niall knew. He felt something lurch in his stomach.

David held his head, then lowered his hands, revealing a ravaged expression about the eyes. "You may be right."

Niall fought back tears of relief. Even a short custodial sentence would satisfy the needs of justice. He hardly heard David's reference to mitigating circumstances. He almost felt grateful and indeed made some conciliatory remark to the effect that Mark would still be a young man after he paid his debt.

"No," David said.

"No what?"

"He won't do any time. None."

"What are you talking about…?"

"It would be too hard for him."

"That's his problem."

David shook his head. "He won't go to jail," he said with all the finality of fact.

"No one is above the law." Niall pointed out sharply.

"Not exactly true," David said. "Diplomats

are the exception."

Struck by a fear that, despite all his planning, he might just have missed something, Niall blurted, "You're bluffing."

"No. I wouldn't have admitted anything if it was a bluff. I just didn't want you to waste any more time trying to wear me down. A criminal prosecution is out of the question. You'd do the same in my shoes." He didn't slur a syllable; his ability to sober up was astonishing.

"There's no way you can hide behind that," Niall grated, but a seed of doubt had lodged in his mind and all the uncertainty of his early years came flooding back.

"I know it's unfair. But when it comes to protecting one's family…" David raised his hands and let them fall back into his lap.

"You can't walk away from this."

"I can." He fumbled in his wallet, produced his Diplomatic Identity Card and read from it, 'The person of a diplomatic agent shall be inviolable. He shall not be liable to any form of arrest or detention … He shall enjoy immunity from the criminal jurisdiction of the receiving State." He paused for a moment and added, "I recently established that this immunity extends to family members. I discussed it with the ambassador that morning you followed me…"

Niall didn't hear him anymore. The rage he felt was due mainly to his own stupidity and had no outlet. He stumbled blindly out of the house and walked for a long time, gasping for air. Tears of frustration scalded his eyes.

When he got home eventually Rona was in bed but still awake. She knew at once that something was wrong and managed to piece together his incoherent account of what had happened.

"We should have known," she repeated over and over. "It's not the first time diplomats in this city have gotten away with…"

"Murder," he finished it for her. "Christ, I can't believe it … I should never have … Your way was best…"

"No, that wouldn't have worked either."

He sat on the edge of the bed, weeping. "Ros … I've failed her… I couldn't even do this … not even a semblance of justice."

"You tried, Niall, you tried everything … It's not your fault."

He shook his head, dismissing all forms of consolation, rejecting the idea that there were no options left. There had to be something.

He went to the State Department on Monday morning. At first a receptionist tried to get him to make an appointment for some time in the future but Niall insisted on seeing a senior official right there and then. He said the matter was extremely urgent. After a long wait in a hall of marble pillars he met the Chief of Protocol, who listened to him in silence and then confirmed the worst. Depending on the weight of evidence the most they could do would be to request the British Foreign Office to repatriate the miscreant family.

"Repatriation?" Niall repeated. "His son killed our only daughter. He admitted it."

"That may be true, Mr. Grenham, but diplomatic immunity is a reciprocal arrangement. The very same immunities are extended to our diplomats abroad. The US cannot take unilateral action."

"I always thought the US was a republic," Niall said with unconcealed bitterness. "This 'arrangement' as you call it is a remnant of imperialism. It is wrong, completely wrong. It goes against the Constitution, against everything the Founding Fathers believed…"

"I'm sorry, Mr. Grenham, there is nothing we can do. Even to press for repatriation might be difficult because of the good relationship that exists between America and Britain right now."

"Because they help us bomb the Arabs." Niall looked at the stars and stripes that decorated the wall behind the Chief of Protocol. "The land of the free," he said, "run by fascists and bully boys."

CHAPTER 18

THE INCIDENT WITH THE POLICE hadn't really scared Mark. He'd been too stoned to understand the gravity or feel the degradation of what had happened. In many ways it was a blast and he knew that the reason the cops let him out the next morning was because they had established who he was. If he learnt any lesson it was that he had a certain amount of clout and was free to go his own way.

Losing his job, however, was something of a problem because he was now contributing very little to the rent. This was a bone of contention since Sue knew he had hidden reserves of cash which he refused to draw on, not for rent in any case.

For his part, David had a lot of thinking to do and he finally decided on *voluntary* repatriation. From a professional point of view he had known for some time that his days in Washington were done; he was no longer on the A team and had become a time-server. He also knew that word of Mark's misdemeanour would soon spread through McLean. It could even get into the *Post*, a paper which lost no opportunity to score points off the diplomatic community. But he wasn't ready to retire – in fact the prospect did not appeal to him at all – so he put himself on the transfer list and hoped for a new posting after some leave which he would take as soon as possible and spend in London.

He explained most of this to Mark on his next visit to New York. Mark made some protest but it seemed to Sue to be no more than a token objection. She said as much and, sensing the beginning of a squabble, David absented himself, saying he would leave them alone for a while.

"It's fine for you to fuck off to London when it suits," Sue complained. "What about me?"

"I've been draining the kitty," Mark pointed out. "You said as much yourself only yesterday."

"Yeah, but you could get another job or break open that piggy bank of yours … Or get another cheque from that Niall character."

"How did you know…?" he began, then changed tack. "It's better this way, Sue, for both of us." The idea of leaving began to grow on him. He would have to forge new contacts in London but at least he would be free of bad memories and the risk of prosecution.

"Jesus, you're some piece of work," Sue spat out. "I always knew you were cheap and self-centred but…"

"Come on, we weren't going anywhere and you knew it." He had visions of their rough sex. He had bruises to show for it; no doubt she had too. And he really had enough of the pigsty they lived in.

"You never gave it, gave us, a chance. You used me."

Her moral indignation amused him. "It takes two to tango."

They were still wrangling when David returned. To his annoyance, she drew him into it as if he were a referee who was bound to rule in her favour.

"It was hardly a relationship made in heaven," David said in a bored tone of voice. As far as he was concerned the only thing they ever had in common was substance abuse, and her hard-done-by act left him cold. It wouldn't have surprised him if she'd claimed to have given Mark the best years of her life. Although still a young woman, she had the makings, he thought, of a mature clinging vine.

"You can't say that," she countered, "We had a lot going here. Mark, say something. I helped you out. I was there for you."

"Well, I don't deny…" he began uncertainly.

"You can't deny it because it's true." Her voice began to tremble.

David was reluctant to listen to any further debate. He gave her a cheque made out to cash which he reckoned would feed her habit for a month or so.

"What good is this to me?" she asked but her tone was not as strident as it was before, and tailed off as she looked at the amount.

Mark packed his few belongings and hesitated over the memorabilia Niall had given him.

"Leave it," David said irritably.

"I don't want it," Sue said with a huff. "I've no room for that junk."

"Then throw it out." David saw that Mark was torn as if it had some weird hold on him. He bustled his son towards the door. Mark resisted and went to embrace Sue but she turned her back on him. "Fuck off," she said tearfully. And that was how they parted.

On the way downstairs David asked if she knew the full story.

"Most of it, I guess," Mark said. "Is that a problem?"

"Blackmail."

"She wouldn't…"

"Oh no? With a habit like hers?" David was exaggerating for his son's benefit. Even if she tried something like that, diplomatic immunity would still protect them. In any case she had no credibility, and would probably end up on a slab in a morgue in a few years' time.

Mark had a sudden memory of being driven around some strange city with his father. He remembered the crush of traders, the hazy heat, spicy smells, and outlines of what he later knew to be minarets. His father drove quickly, hunched over the wheel. He had a vague sense that maybe he had run away and been found by his father. He didn't probe the memory any further but rummaged in his bag to make sure for the third or fourth time that he hadn't left his stash behind. Sue would be OK, she had a float and had other ways of making money. She would take up again with the crowd she used to run with. It would all be OK.

Niall got in his car and drove to the bend in Kirby road where he pulled over and parked, though did not switch off the ignition. Through the trees he could see the oncoming traffic and hear the noise of engines grow and diminish according to distance. He stayed for a long time, clutching the steering wheel. He noticed that the back of one hand was bleeding profusely and he had no idea why. Cars passed in both directions, many of the drivers giving him questioning or hostile looks. He worried as the light began to fade and turn into mist; this was not planned for and the lack of visibility would make the manoeuvre much more difficult than he'd realised. As soon as the jeep rounded the bend he would move out; Mark would be in the passenger seat. Niall would have to accelerate quickly from a standing start; that was why he kept the engine running. He would have no more than a few seconds to get his speed up. If he struck the jeep towards the rear it would slew across the road into the buttressed bridge that spanned a tributary of the Potomac.

Time passed slowly and the mist swirled around even the lowest branches of the trees. He pressed the accelerator to reassure himself that the engine was running. He had never felt so alert and could almost sense the collision. He longed for it and the annihilation it would bring. Destruction followed by peace.

When he finally saw the jeep approach he didn't hesitate, but revved hard and shot the car forward. Just before the impact he saw that Ros was driving the jeep. And he couldn't stop. It was too late … Fear stayed with him long after he woke and jumped from the armchair in which he had dozed off. Wide-eyed, he stared at familiar objects in the room.

David put the keys of the jeep in an envelope for the movers. They would ship it to Southampton along with his furniture which filled less than two containers. Without any real regret or nostalgia he took a last look at the timber-frame house with its Cape Cod shutters and portico. He would miss the pool, nothing else. Leaving the office had been done with equal dispatch although there had been a few drinks in the ambassador's office, a restrained speech or two and a ripple of applause. He knew that most of his colleagues were glad to see the back of him and he couldn't blame Mark entirely for that. But he was damned if he would undergo a similar lukewarm ritual with the neighbours. They could all go to hell, as far as he was concerned.

So, after he'd checked his briefcase for tickets, passports and money, he and Mark sat into a taxi and headed for Dulles airport. There was little conversation though Mark did ask what London would be like – he had only the vaguest recollection of it. David couldn't enlighten him very much, even if he wanted to; he himself hadn't been back in years.

On the way out to the aircraft in the mobile lounge he noticed how Mark had begun to fidget, kneading his hands and touching his face. It was annoying and pathetic at the same time. What was going to become of him? He seemed to have no control over his life and the prospect of getting him into a detox programme was receding.

During the flight David reviewed the options. He didn't relish the idea of staying with his sister and thought it would be better to move into guest quarters or a self-catering hotel, if such facilities were available in London. He also thought about his next assignment; it would probably be a hardship post to teach him a lesson – the father paying for the sins of the son. The voluntary nature of the repatriation was little more than a technicality. His masters at the Foreign Office would know the full story. Alternatively, they might give him a list of hardship posts and let him stick a pin in it. It didn't matter a great deal either way. One place was much the same as another and the city of his birth had no special allure.

Mark mellowed out during the flight and paid frequent trips to the lavatory. David reckoned he was nipping from a flask or popping some low-grade pills, anything to give him a charge. He could understand the occasional need for a hair of the dog but this constant topping up was beyond his ken. He kept his own counsel, however, not wishing to create a scene in public, but he wondered where and how it would all end.

CHAPTER 19

IT WAS RONA who first saw the movers clearing out David's house. She had a word with the workmen and established that David and his son had already left and that the furniture and jeep were being shipped to a warehouse in Southampton.

Seen through a front window, the suddenly vacated rooms looked cavernous and bleak. One of the workmen told her with a grin that he'd never before come across such a mountain of empty liquor bottles. With uncanny accuracy he opined that the previous occupant must've been a diplomat.

As she re-crossed the road, Rona had to stop to let a kid on roller blades pass. He leant from one side to the other, mimicking a kind of slalom action and for a moment she admired his easy grace. For that same moment everything seemed normal, just as it should be.

"Gone?" Niall repeated that evening. "Just like that?" He didn't know what to make of it all. His fawn-coloured trench coat lay across his knees. Hamm, the Spaniel, repeatedly head-butted his shins, angling to be taken for a walk.

"Good riddance," she said. "We'll never have to see them again." She noticed that he was still wrestling with it and tried to help him come to a conclusion. "It's an admission, almost a confession. People will be able to put two and two together…"

"It's not good enough. Nowhere near…" Absent-mindedly he patted the dog, who became more optimistic about his chances of getting out.

"I know, Niall, but there's nothing we can do about it." She paused and bent over him, noticing how much he had aged. "Can you accept it?"

He looked up sideways and slowly shook his head.

"We have to go on with … our lives." She shrugged in apology for putting themselves first.

He stared at the dog as if seeing him for the first time. Gone. They were gone, father and son, leaving nothing, not a trace. They came, killed and disappeared.

Rona knelt beside the chair, putting her face at a level with his. "If it's a matter of … closure, that will come in time."

"No, god damn it." He bridled suddenly. "Justice must mean something. We're supposed to be living in a civilised country."

She held his hand to stop him crumpling the coat in his lap. "We're not going to get justice. Try to accept it, Niall. You must try."

"Can you settle for that?"

"In time, I hope … Ros is gone. Locking up Mark won't alter that fact. Try to forget about him."

He turned towards her in amazement. How could she say that or even think it? It was pure rationalisation. If it helped her, so be it. But he couldn't buy into it, not for a second. And he never would.

He finally brought the dog for a walk, studiously avoiding the Highsmith house. Hamm seemed to enjoy these irregular and more frequent walks and scampered happily about, sniffing the hedgerows and tree trunks. At one point he carried a stick in his jaws and laid it at his master's feet, quivering in anticipation. Niall threw it with no great enthusiasm. Hamm leapt twisting in mid-air, caught it cleanly and brought it proudly back, hoping for a reprise.

From the door Rona watched them for a while and wondered if hiring Diane had been such a bright idea. What good had the discovery done them? What good was knowledge on its own without the possibility of action, and what effect was it having on her husband? He seemed so distant and absorbed these days. It wasn't just his tendency towards introspection that worried her but the risk that his health might suffer. And he wasn't the type to ask for help. While they had communicated to some degree, she still hadn't had the opportunity to talk to him in the way Betty had suggested.

As he turned the corner into Loch Raven Drive he virtually bumped into Si and Betty. There was embarrassment all round.

"Great dog that." Si patted the bobbing head of the spaniel then thumped his own chest to indicate the bracing quality of the air which, on the verge of autumn, was almost breathable.

Betty was more direct. "We only just heard

… And we saw the removal vans. They've skipped, haven't they? You never know people, do you? You just never know."

"Some neighbours, huh. Vipers in our bosom, if you ask me." Si tried to help her out.

"And that diplomatic immunity business … It's outrageous. You must feel … If it happened to me I'd feel so … cheated." She shook her head in sympathy.

Si nodded in agreement. Betty had a great instinct for saying the right thing. He wouldn't go far wrong by endorsing her views in situations like this.

"Yes, it's hard not to feel that," Niall answered. He valued friendship and knew they were trying to help, but for some reason he would have preferred to be on his own with the dog.

Betty didn't leave before expressing the desire to see him and Rona more frequently on the golf course. In her book golf was a cure for most ills, especially worry, which she regarded as a potentially deadly ailment, indulged in by weak-willed people.

"They've deepened the pot bunker on the fifth," Si added by way of inducement. "It's murder now." Instinctively, he squared his stance and started to grip an imaginary sand wedge. Oblivious of his *faux pas*, he repeated his wife's prescription, adding that Niall was probably under-golfed.

As they parted, it occurred to Niall that he

and Rona hadn't played the damned game in ages. During their last outing she had been upset by the appearance of a deer on one of the fairways. As a child Ros had always been a willing caddy, hoping that one or more of the deer that inhabited the bordering woodland would make an appearance during the round. She had been so drawn to animals they were convinced she would become a vet or a zoologist when she grew up. The frequent sight of road-kill on Old Kirby used to upset her greatly. And she had loved Hamm who, in his quieter moments, lying down outside her bedroom door, still clearly pined for her.

No doubt Rona was haunted by these and other memories and there were probably times when avoidance seemed the better course. He knew that she often worked late and attended buyers' conventions which a year ago she'd have gladly delegated for the sake of family life.

Niall wondered if he had changed in any noticeable way – apart from taking more frequent walks with the dog. He was vaguely conscious of being moodier and of alternating, for no apparent reason, between deep sadness and sudden squalls of anger. Sometimes, he was angry with himself for various reasons, including his failure to anticipate David Highsmith's diplomatic trump card. There had been other widely reported cases in the past, not only in Washington but also in New York – where UN diplomats had been involved. He should have been alert to the danger. Despite all the psychological warfare he'd planned and executed, he had missed the wood for the trees. How they must be laughing now, knowing they had a safety net all along.

He hoped that Rona and he would not drift further apart. He didn't know where the limits were but had some instinct that they were close to the edge as things stood. He needed her more than ever, but there was some compulsion in him that was often frightening in its intensity, and it formed a barrier between them because it was not shared by her. At night he would sometimes wake up from a bad dream, his eyes opening slowly to stare at the ceiling. He would lie on his back grinding his teeth until it was time to get up.

The sky became greyer as evening closed in. He put the leash on Hamm, who accepted it without a protest. They retraced their steps, again avoiding the empty Highsmith house.

In early fall Rona was surprised when he announced that he felt in need of a break and was considering a visit to Dublin for about a fortnight or so.

"I know I've been a pain in the neck," he said, "but I'll be able to sort myself out over there, see some friends, like Gerry Connolly…"

"Your old school pal? It's a great idea," she enthused. "Of course, I'll be busy with the fall collection." She laid down the pruning shears and shaded her eyes against the sun which shone through the greenhouse.

"Oh."

"You don't sound terribly disappointed." She laughed suddenly. "It's OK. We'll do something together later. Go for it. Come back refreshed." She felt relieved that he was at last planning to do something.

"Never knew you were so understanding." The ease of the transaction – for that is what it was – and his own glibness made him feel guilty. But the die was cast; there was no going back.

A week earlier he had called the British Embassy and asked for David. A secretary told him he'd demitted office and gone home. Niall interpreted this to mean London and was greatly surprised when the girl charmingly volunteered the information that David had been assigned to Dublin.

"You know, the Republic of Ireland," she added, to clear up any residual misunderstanding. "You'd have to call the embassy there to get his home address."

"Do you happen to know if he brought his son, Mark, with him? He's my godson, you know."

"I believe so."

"Thank you, thank you very much."

CHAPTER 20

AT THE AIRPORT Rona gave him a peck on the cheek as he went into the departure area. Through the glass partition she watched him go through security, failing the metal detector and raising his arms to be frisked. He looked back once and waved.

Shortly after take-off the stewardess offered him a sticker that he could fix to the top of the seat if he wanted to skip the meal and sleep instead. He accepted one but in the event he couldn't sleep. The drone of the plane was like a trajectory that stretched ahead. His course was set.

He had reached the stage where he could not distinguish justice from revenge and it made no difference to him. The pain that enveloped him left no room for scruples, or fears. Nor did consequences matter, any more than they mattered to a dumb animal stampeding away from fire. He had to be rid of that slow-burning, relentless pain. But unlike a stricken animal he had the ability and will to plan for deliverance in the most effective way. Time was not an issue; he could make haste slowly. This was reinforced by the small relief he felt at having taken the first step.

The hours passed slowly then suddenly they broke cloud cover and there was Dublin Bay just ahead with its small satellite islands, broken headlands and the lighthouses of Howth and Dún Laoghaire. It seemed to have been waiting for him all those years. Niall had forgotten how startlingly green and fresh it all was. A little later he could see the Liffey snaking through the city, that ordinary drab, khaki-coloured river, Anna Livia, made remarkable by myth – the sow that ate her farrow and perhaps also made him a spoiled priest, too full of doubts to justify himself to his calling. How ironic that seemed now with the clergy in the dock for so many misdemeanours and crimes and he, himself, embarked on one.

He was close to home and yet further away than ever. In the airport he heard all those familiar accents and idioms, less brash than those in the States. Yet he knew the barbs those softer voices could conceal. Still waters, *uisce fé talamh*. Much was hidden here, repressed by authority; jokes could kill, silences maim. He went to the bathroom then joined a queue for taxis.

About an hour later, having been brought up to date on the intricacies of Irish politics by a taxi driver, Niall checked into a hotel near Stillorgan. He had a bath and went to bed early but woke in the middle of the night and paced the room which gave a moonlit view of the running track at Belfield. When he was in Maynooth they sometimes competed there. Healthy pursuits for seminarians, the spiritual seed corn of the nation. They wore black shorts and strip for modesty.

After one event in which he managed to avoid finishing last, the House Master called him over and suggested that in future he might consider wearing an athletic supporter. The seminarians kept very much to themselves and were discouraged from mixing with UCD louts. They were a select band called by god. Those were the days when the whole country was going through puberty and when it finally grew up the old order was gone and the select band was consigned to the scrap heap. Niall of course had bailed out long before that happened.

After a light breakfast he went to the lobby and hired a car. He wasn't exactly sure why but felt he would need the flexibility a car offered. Maybe he had become an American after all. People used to snigger at American tourists; now he was one, totally dependent on modern conveniences. He reminded himself to call Rona later in the day; she would want to know he'd arrived safely. His mother had been the same. Arriving safely was the main thing; it apparently didn't matter if you dropped dead the next day.

He drove into the city centre; the omphalos was marked by the gleaming spire that extended into the clouds. He had always liked its simplicity and wondered if it might have been designed to symbolise the Dubliner's desire to puncture pomposity. There were so many new shopping centres, arcades, fast-food places, ritzy pubs and nightclubs which, combined with teeming youth, made him disposed to believe

what he'd read in the in-flight magazine about
Dublin being the leisure capital of Europe.

He drove aimlessly for a while, welcoming
the crush of traffic because it gave him a chance
to look around. He bought a few items, including
an umbrella and a tweed cap, in a shopping
centre at the top of Grafton Street. Then he called
Rona at Bloomingdales, sensing from her
manner that she was busy and probably had some
people in her office. She told him to enjoy the
break, not to drink too much Guinness and to
bring back a side of smoked salmon. He gave her
the name and number of his hotel in Stillorgan.

After a cup of coffee in Bewleys – still the
old-fashioned emporium he remembered with
fondness – he went back to the Stephen's Green
carpark and headed south. On the Merrion Road
he passed the new British Embassy, a long low
Scandinavian-style building that was completely
out of sympathy with its surroundings. He
recalled how the original embassy had been
burned down after Bloody Sunday, how the
police had wisely refrained from intervening. A
friend of his, a peaceable man, had joined the
angry throng and, for want of anything better,
had hurled expensive golf balls at the windows
of the burning building. Those rebels-for-a-day
had long since gone back to their comfortable,
constitutional lives, forgetting all about the
bloodletting in Northern Ireland in those terrible
years. Despite the Good Friday Agreement, he
wondered if Catholics had ever really achieved

'parity of esteem' without which he thought peace could only be skin-deep. He knew that Brexit had, unfortunately, awakened old antagonisms.

"You old codger." Gerry Connolly appeared from behind a pillar in the lobby of the hotel. He was grey and balding but had the same slack grin that Niall remembered from school. It used to get him into trouble with the Brothers, who thought he was being sarcastic. He used to sit in the desk behind Niall and often threatened to prod him with the sharp end of a compass if he didn't help him with his algebra. But it was Gerry who'd braved the wrath of a sadistic brother by coming to Niall's rescue that time he'd been locked in the cupboard for failing to rattle off the months of the year in Irish.

They shook hands and embraced – briefly and a little self-consciously.

"It's good to see you after all this time," Niall said. "I'm sorry we missed you when you were over."

"Get out of this kip of a hotel and come and stay at my place."

"I couldn't impose."

"Don't be daft. I'm still a bachelor. I've loads of room. If you turn a blind eye to the mess we'll be grand."

Niall finally agreed when he gauged the conviction in Gerry's voice and manner. He packed up and paid the bill. Gerry also had a car and he led the way further south to a suburban area just past Dún Laoghaire. The house was a well-appointed semi with a view of the Wicklow hills on one side and at least a corner of the bay on the other.

In the higgledy-piggledy lounge they conversed and drank late into the night, catching up on old times. Niall appreciated the company more than he realised. Since leaving school Gerry had done several completely unrelated jobs ranging from ship's cook to boxing coach. He had once had a tentative association with the Provisional IRA which he managed to break when he became sickened by the indiscriminate violence.

"I'm still a nationalist though," he pointed out. "Unfortunately, people assume that that makes you a mad bomber. But you know what's really awful about the whole situation?"

Niall shook his head.

"Violence does work. All the official pundits reject that notion. They have to. But look at the record. The UK used violence against this country for hundreds of years. Stormont used institutional violence for as long as they had the whip hand. The British used it when they had to. And the Provos knew damn well that it's the only way to get leverage. The media doesn't really care about civil rights but when a bomb goes off they sit up and take notice. A couple of bombs in the City of London brought the British to the negotiating table. Power is the only thing that works and violence is the only power the minority has. The squeaky wheel gets the oil. That's the truth of the matter, though no one will admit it."

"It doesn't say much for human nature." Niall remembered the one and only time he'd lost his temper. Having been humiliated by a bully, he went into a blind rage and struck out wildly in all directions, completely devoid of fear, and managed to land a couple of lucky punches. He felt sick to his stomach afterwards. But the bully never bothered him again.

"We hear a lot about empowerment these days," Gerry said. "If it's not given voluntarily it'll be seized by violent methods. That's what the Provos were about. Much as I hate to admit it, logic was on their side. I'm afraid they might mobilise again in the wake of that damn Brexit business and the new border. "

"I'm not up to speed on any of that." Niall didn't want to pursue the matter, maybe because he had become an underdog so recently, deprived of a basic right. It was all too close for comfort. "I must say you've done a lot of interesting jobs in your time."

"I met some characters all right," Gerry conceded. "Fell into bad company too. Which is maybe why I never settled down." He lay back, glass in hand, and rested his feet on the coffee table which, judging by the scored surface, had often served as a footstool.

"Regrets?"

"Yes and no. I do miss kids. I've plenty of

nieces and nephews though. Aw, hell, I don't expect too much out of life these days. Keep your sights low and you won't be disappointed."

"I know that feeling." As the night wore on Niall became more and more talkative and found himself revealing things that he had kept to himself. Gerry was certainly a good listener but it was more than that. School days had somehow built up a legacy of trust. They hadn't met in over thirty years but whatever bonds had originally been formed had not been weakened by neglect. He remembered Gerry being so quick and sharp at maths. He could solve problems without using x and y – no one ever knew how – but the teacher gave him no credit for that, and so a natural talent went untapped.

As dawn began to filter in through the thin curtains of the front room Niall realised with some surprise that he had told Gerry almost everything. It didn't bother him, however; the question of trust simply didn't arise.

"I don't think you're cut out for this, Niall."

"It has to be me. There's no one else."

"It's going to cut you to the quick."

"Dig two graves and all that? I don't care … Nothing matters to me any more. It's like what you said earlier about not expecting much. I don't expect anything. Not now. For a while, before … life was wonderful. It was a surprising second chance given to me after I left the seminary. But it was too good to last. That's all changed." It occurred to him that the action he had in mind could well be a substitute for suicide.

"Would Ros want you to do this?" Gerry looked steadily at him.

"Probably not. But I have to do it."

"You're sure? Absolutely sure?"

Niall nodded slowly.

Later they dozed off where they sat. Niall was the first to wake and he looked around the strange room in confusion until he got his bearings. After a while the surroundings seemed familiar; he almost felt at home.

Gerry was sprawled on a Dralon-covered couch opposite him snoring softly. Niall went out to the kitchen where the sun shone weakly through the Venetian blinds, and made tea and toast. He brought a tray back into the lounge where Gerry was beginning to wake up, albeit with some difficulty.

"Ah, god bless." He sniffed the warm brew. "Good man yourself." He drank the tea with even more relish than the Powers Gold Label some hours earlier. He peered over the rim of the cup. "It wasn't just the drink talking last night?"

"No," Niall said.

"I thought not."

CHAPTER 21

IT WAS IN that Scandinavian-style building on the Merrion Road that David had first reported for duty. The ambassador, knowing the circumstances and feeling he had been sold a pup, gave him a rather tepid welcome and the briefest introduction to the rest of the staff. He himself had been given Dublin after his heart attack to allow him glide gracefully and without stress into a well-earned retirement. Then Brexit struck and he found himself busier than ever. As one Tory Minister put it, there was a danger that Ireland would become the tail wagging the British dog. The last thing he needed was a disgraced and burnt-out assistant.

He lent David his own driver to help him move with this delinquent son into an embassy house on the Vico Road near Killiney. It was a very fine Victorian house set well back from the road, surrounded by eucalyptus trees, monkey puzzle and a high granite wall. There were astonishing views of the bay and Dalkey Island. For the first time David felt his heart lift, though not for long.

"I'm not living in this mausoleum," Mark announced straight off the bat. They were standing in a large panelled hallway that resonated to the sounds of a grandfather clock. The smell of furniture polish and linseed oil was overpowering.

"I hardly think you're in a position to pick and choose." David knew immediately what lay behind Mark's desire to go off on his own. This was not the new beginning he might have hoped for; in fact he could imagine the awful cycle beginning all over again.

"I have money," Mark said. There was something left in his trust and he still had about a third of the cash Niall had given him. "And I can get a job."

"And mess it up like you did in New York."

"I explained all that. It wasn't my fault. Those Italians were impossible. Jesus, talk about a bunch of hotheads. It'll be OK here in this backwater."

"How is it that nothing is ever your fault?" David wondered why he bothered. Was it possible that Mark drifted in and out of a delusional state? He doubted it because there were times when he displayed extraordinary cunning. "Look, stay here for a week. Then we'll talk about it again."

Mark shrugged as if to indicate he had no great objection to the proposal.

But two days later he was gone, taking all the spare cash he could find in the house as well as a Georgian silver tea service. He found a bedsitter closer to town. There was nothing David could do but he resolved not to provide any money after Mark's ran out. 'Tough love' was the only bit of psycho-babble he could accept as having any connection with common sense.

Having visited the garment district in New York and attended several fashion shows, Rona began to put her ideas together. With Niall away she didn't mind working late; in fact it was better than going home to an empty house. When she was ready with her recommendations for the fall collection she made her pitch in the form of a Powerpoint presentation to the Group Policy Committee which was chaired by one of the senior Vice Presidents. It went well and the committee gave her a spontaneous round of applause.

Afterwards the VP followed her out and walked her back to the office.

"Great pitch, Rona," he said. "Excellent selections. I think they'll do very well."

"But?" She sounded like Niall, looking for the downside. On the other hand the VP was known to be effusive and one had to take his compliments with a grain of salt. Nevertheless, she was badly shaken by what he, eventually and with much evasion, suggested to her, namely that she might begin to consider moving to a more advisory position.

"I'm not sure … I understand."

"We need your input, Rona. That goes without saying. You have a great eye for fashion and can combine that with the corporate ethos.

It's a rare combination, believe me, and we're lucky to have you on our side. What I'm saying is that your value to the group would be enhanced further in a consultancy role. The younger buyers could learn a great deal from you."

In the middle of all the corporate speak three words stood out: advisory, consultancy and younger. She was being kicked upstairs. Decision-making and negotiating functions were being taken away from her. She didn't have to parse it any further, and to seek additional clarification would embarrass them both. Maybe she was making it too easy for him but dignity was important to her.

She felt drained that evening when she got home. It occurred to her that they might already have chosen her replacement – possibly Lorna Baldwin, a graduate in design, who was no more than twenty-five and who had done well with teen-wear over the last few seasons. Was this another rite of passage looming up, Rona wondered. If it was to be her Indian summer could the menopause be far behind? She missed Ros so much. It was at times like these that Ros would come up with the gesture or phrase that would put everything in perspective. They would probably end up having a good laugh about it.

She couldn't sleep that night and at about two a.m. she went down to the kitchen for a glass of milk; from there she phoned Niall. The receptionist told her that he had checked out of the hotel the previous day. Rona wondered why he had done that and why he hadn't told her; it just wasn't like him.

"You don't have to do this," Niall said.

"I'll get you started. Anyway your accent isn't up to par yet." Gerry grinned and went out to the phone in the hall. He rang the British embassy and asked to speak to Mr. Highsmith. When David came on the line he said, "Sorry to disturb you, sir. This is Sergeant Murray here, Store Street Garda Station. We picked up your son, Mark, some time ago."

"Is he OK?" David asked.

"Yes, sir. But he's the worse for wear, if you know what I mean."

"I believe I do, unfortunately."

"We don't need to detain him. But for some reason he won't give us his home address, which is needed…"

"I'll send a car round for him," David said.

Gerry thought quickly. "If you don't mind me saying so, I think that would be a mistake. It would make life a little too easy for him. It would be more … salutary if we drove him home in a squad car." Gerry had a pencil at the ready, waiting for the address.

"Thanks, but that won't be necessary, Sergeant. I'll have a car around in twenty minutes. Store Street you say?" David rang off.

Gerry went into the kitchen and told Niall it hadn't worked and that questions would be asked when the driver returned to the embassy empty-handed.

"It was still worth a try," David said. With any luck no great damage had been done. David would in all likelihood assume that the Irish police were inefficient and prone to cock-ups.

"He sounds a bit of a bollocks." Gerry scraped burnt toast into the sink and searched the fridge for a jar of marmalade. "If the son is the same I wouldn't like to meet him on a dark night." He looked at Niall. "What now? Plan B?"

"I don't want to involve you any more in this."

"I'll help you locate the little bastard. After that you're on your own." He gave him a knowing look. "Assuming you want to take it further."

Because of the bus lane on the Merrion Road they had to park right up on the footpath and were an obvious target for traffic wardens and clampers. The chosen spot was at least a hundred metres north of the Embassy and its security cameras, but it did give them an oblique view of the main gate.

"Are you going for the doughnuts?" Gerry asked.

"What?"

"You know. Cops on a stakeout."

Niall managed a tight grin; none of this seemed real and yet it was far from being a fantasy.

At about four-thirty the diplomatic staff started to file out of the building. Not unexpectedly, David was in the vanguard and for one second Niall thought he looked across the street straight at him, but it was probably his imagination. As soon as he emerged from the carpark Niall put the hired car into gear and followed him. The car in front was a brand new Jaguar, which indicated that David had got rid of the jeep. He was probably trying to expunge the record and to make a fresh start. Easy for him, Niall thought, although perhaps not as easy as he might wish.

Both cars became embroiled in a tailback from the Blackrock bypass and had to slow to a crawl. At Seapoint they took the coast road, which was moving more freely. David had obviously learned the rat-running techniques of South Dublin commuters very quickly. They had to go inland again at Sandycove but after Dalkey they moved back to the coast road. A little later the Jag turned into a large gateway with stone lions on the piers. There was a rattle of a cattle grid, then the gates closed electronically.

"So this is the house." Niall brought the car to a halt and undid his seat belt.

"A mansion more like," Gerry said. "They live well, these diplomats. I wonder if the son is staying with him."

As he switched off the ignition Niall eyed the perimeter wall which was daunting though not impossible. If he could get over it the trees would give plenty of cover, allowing him to get quite near the house to look for signs of a second occupant.

Gerry dismissed the notion, arguing that neither of them was in the first flush of youth and could damage a ligament or worse. In any case, CCTV cameras were likely to be a problem. He had a better idea. At his bidding Niall drove around Killiney Hill and parked outside the Druid's Chair. He waited while Gerry went into a small house in the village to chat up the local postman. When he returned they both went into the pub, which at that hour was almost empty. The barman spent most of his time bringing crates up from the cellar and re-stocking the shelves behind the counter.

The visit to the postman had paid dividends; Mr. Highsmith Junior had been in the house for two days and then moved out.

"That figures," Niall said. "He doesn't know his new address, I suppose."

"No. That's going to be your big problem. It sounds like he's gone to ground."

At least they'd achieved something, Niall thought. He wondered if the abortive phone call might have put David on the alert. Suppose he called a mutual acquaintance in Washington and discovered that Niall had gone to Dublin – possible but unlikely. One way of minimising that possibility would be to tip Rona off, but how could he do that without revealing his hand? Better to sit tight.

Gerry broke in on his thoughts, "If he's a dope fiend like you say, he might be knocking around the Rathmines area."

"Flatland." Niall remembered the cramped, damp bedsitters that weren't fit for human habitation though were deemed perfectly suitable for students.

"The very place. Though it's more sophisticated nowadays. A lot of the heroin that's smuggled in through West Cork gets distributed there by a nasty piece of work called Stuke. He thinks Rathmines is his territory."

"You're not talking Mafia here?" Niall asked incredulously.

"No. But it's fairly organised all the same. The Guards – and the Criminal Assets Bureau – have been after Stuke for years but they can't get the goods on him. Years ago the Provos tried to nail him too as a PR stunt but eventually gave up. And the customs men can't cut off the supply of heroin because they haven't the resources to police the coastline around Cork and Kerry."

"Didn't I read somewhere that the real drug problem is in the inner city and on the Northside?"

Gerry nodded but went on to explain that the better-off users from respectable families probably tended to gravitate towards the Rathmines area, which was safer, recently semi-gentrified, and where the merchandise was purer and more reliable. "That's where your man is likely to be."

But where in Rathmines, Niall wondered. He remembered it as a rat's nest of flats and bedsitters where, for tax reasons, the landlords refused to allow tenants to put names or bells on doors and where the tenants themselves tended to move around, squat, sofa-surf, and do moonlight flits. There was only one way he could find out and it wasn't going to be easy or risk-free. He outlined a plan of sorts. Gerry agreed that it probably was the only way but tried for the last time to talk him out of the whole enterprise. Eventually, he gave him the name of a pub, O'Toole's, which was rumoured to be one of Stuke's watering holes. He gave him the names of a couple of minor players who drank in O'Toole's and advised him to be subtle and careful; if he came on strong it could all blow up in his face. He also told him his accent needed a little more work. They embraced and Niall thanked him for his help. Gerry wished him well and told him to contact him, day or night, if he needed to.

Not surprisingly, there was very little for David to do in his new posting and time lay heavy on his hands. Whitehall had little of any interest in the Irish economy now that the more colourful days of the Celtic Tiger were past history, and the ambassador wouldn't let him next or near anything connected with the EU, Brexit or bilateral trade arrangements. None of these exclusions bothered David unduly but he found it ironic that he no longer had to avoid work for the simple reason that none came his way.

By his demeanour and in other less subtle ways, the ambassador let him know as often as he could that he regarded him as a disgrace to the profession. For his part David regarded His Excellency as a grammar-school boy scout who seemed to believe that diplomacy actually achieved things, that it served a purpose beyond itself. Of course enthusiasm and blind loyalty paid off in the promotion stakes. The trouble was he couldn't quite tell whether the ambassador was faking or not. Maybe he was a true believer, a self-deluded soul who swallowed whole the lumpless pablum of the Foreign Office.

Apart from his new house there was little about Dublin he liked. It may have had a certain raw energy that no doubt appealed to younger people but for the older, more jaded palate it had little to offer. And its lived-in quality which others found quaint left him cold. He could do without the repetitive jigging music that issued from every second pub, the Liffey smells (which suggested raw sewage to him), the epidemic litter and exhaust fumes. And of course the city had no clout whatsoever in the geo-political sphere. He knew that the few contacts he had left in London were laughing up their cuffs at his posting. He had drawn the short straw, thanks to Mark.

He was at his desk reading the *Times* (London) when his secretary buzzed through.

"What is it, Kate?"

"Two items, Mr. Highsmith. I've had a call from the CEO of a firm in Galway asking for a list of bicycle manufacturers in the UK."

"Wonderful. If he rings again put him on to the Commercial Section. What else?"

"One of the drivers left a message for you. He said Mark wasn't at Store Street and the Guards … Police … knew nothing about it. Does that make any sense to you?"

"Yes and no." He swept the newspapers off his desk. "Tell the driver I want to see him."

CHAPTER 22

IT WAS A SELLERS' market, so Niall had to pay way over the odds for a room in Upper Rathmines Road. It was a bleak place – not yet gentrified or designated for tax breaks – with an electric ring in one corner and a military-style cot in another. He had a cover story to tell the landlord but it wasn't necessary. Once he paid the two months' rent in advance and the damage deposit, the landlord was satisfied. Niall's accent seemed to pass muster.

When he went out into the streets he wore a shabby suit he'd picked up in an Oxfam shop. The area had become quite cosmopolitan since his time. He was struck by the number of young women who could be seen pushing baby strollers in front of them. Single mothers, an elderly woman explained to him, children rearing children, supported by the State. What a sea-change, Niall thought. He could remember a time when a single mother was a pariah, pointed out in the street as an example of evil incarnate. The clergy were so wrong to perpetuate such unChristian values and now they were being hounded by the media, outed as secretly-married men and as paedophiles. They had all but self-destructed. He was glad he'd bailed out when he did. Was it possible that he'd sensed back then where their elitist attitudes would ultimately lead?

Though many of the buildings had changed, Rathmines was still more or less the rabbit warren he remembered. If Georgetown was an elegant reception room for posh guests, Rathmines was the scruffy kitchen where the family gathered for a late night brew. He thought Ros would have liked it warts and all. He had always wanted to bring her to Dublin and she had often reminded him, being particularly keen to see the seminary, but the time was never right.

Later that evening he dropped into O'Toole's bar and lounge. It was an ordinary sort of pub not far from the council flats. It obviously hadn't been decorated for years, nor had it been afflicted with repro furnishings. Through the varnish on the counter old stains and cigarette burns could be seen like fossils in amber. Some old geezers brooded into their pints, and if they were drug barons, Niall was a Dutchman.

He ordered a pint and chatted to the barman who was called Seán. He didn't want to ask too many questions on his first foray. Seán obviously assumed he was passing trade and didn't invest too much time in him, but that was all right for now. After a while Niall brought his drink to the back of the bar and sat at a plain deal table in which the nail heads were visible above the surface of the wood.

With his cap on and an *Evening Herald* opened at the racing page, he thought he blended in well enough. Through an archway to his left he could see a few couples in what passed for a lounge. After an hour or so he noticed a group of men going into a room off the other end of the bar. For the few seconds the door remained open he saw that it was quite a large area with a pool table, and that it was furnished to a much higher standard. He thought that another door led off that room but wasn't certain.

He waited for another hour but no one emerged from the inner sanctum. He thought of putting some more questions to Seán but decided not to rush his fences. After leaving the pub he bought a hamburger from one of the many fast-food places and brought it back to his room. It took him all of five minutes to eat it and dump the greaseproof wrapper in the torn wicker waste bin. Then, regretting his hostility to mobile phones, he gathered up a pocketful of change, went out to the public coin box on the landing and tried to reach Rona. The old vandalised phone gobbled up most of his change but he couldn't get through. Maybe just as well, he thought. She would certainly wonder what all the clicks and pips were about. Resolving to find a more serviceable phone the next day, he went back to his room and went to bed.

He lay awake for a long time on the small cot, listening to the traffic and the chimes of the town-hall clock which boomed out every quarter hour. At about two in the morning he heard a group of revellers, probably students, stumble and laugh on the landing outside his door. It didn't bother him unduly; he didn't need much sleep since Ros died, and in some ways noise was better than silence.

In the morning he boiled water in a saucepan on the gas ring and made a cup of instant coffee. After he left the seminary, a quarter of a century ago, he lived for a while in a room not unlike this one and the discipline of having to fend for himself probably helped him avoid a breakdown. Doing small repetitive chores had its place in the larger scheme of things. Wasn't it Jordan Peterson who advised young Millennials to tidy their rooms before changing the world?

He spent most of the day in the public library which was situated at the back of the town hall. The newspapers carried a fair amount of world news but on the whole were a little parochial. He was struck by the number and scale of crimes and political scandals. Something had changed all right since he'd left Ireland, and not for the better, with the exception of living standards. Was this, he wondered, a case of growing materialism giving rise to a weakening of moral values? And he wasn't overly impressed by the standard of journalism; apart from the odd serious piece that had obviously been cannibalised from web sources, the broadsheets were full of opinion, gossip and agony-aunt columns. They were worse than the tabloids because they pretended to be a cut above them, purveying a kind of middle-class sleaze. He was just about to dip into the latest Sebastian Barry novel when a loud bell sounded. The library was closing early because of budget cuts. The staff repeated the reason several times.

After a bite to eat in an Italian fish and chip shop he walked over to Harold's Cross, pausing at the dog track where, as a kid in short pants, he'd gone on a couple of occasions with his father, who spent more time in the bars than watching the greyhounds. His father's dream of one big win had never materialised and if it had, he'd probably have celebrated until all the money was gone. But he was a colourful character who seized the moment, in contrast to Niall's mother who seemed to invite hardships as if they could be cashed in for a reward in the next life. They never exchanged a cross word, however, having learnt to tolerate their differences, and he remembered them both fondly. His great regret used to be that they hadn't lived long enough to see their granddaughter. Now, he was glad they had passed on before learning of her murder.

A light drizzle began to fall and he retraced his steps along Leinster Road back towards the main drag of Rathmines. He did not rule out the possibility that he might catch a glimpse of Mark in the street and thought it better to spend as much time as he could where the action was. After walking up and down the entire length of Rathmines, investigating shopping malls, garage forecourts and billiard parlours, he went into O'Tooles.

Seán recognised him and Niall spent longer

at the bar talking to him. After the preliminaries were out of the way, he told him he'd lost his job in Britain and had come home to look for work.

"The dole is better here anyway," Seán said, taking a tray of pint glasses out of the washer and stacking them on shelves under the counter.

"The boss over there was a decent skin. It wasn't his fault the business went under." Niall went on to say how the boss's son was a bit wild and had come over to Dublin to do his own thing. The family thought he had a flat somewhere in Rathmines. He gave a description of Mark but it didn't register with Seán who asked if the lad was in trouble.

"Ah no, just a bit headstrong," Niall said. "You know how they are at that age. Not to worry. He'll probably go home when he's good and ready. I just said I'd keep my eyes open while I was over here."

"If I hear anything I'll let you know," Seán promised. "Any kids yourself?"

Niall hesitated. "No."

"You're as well off. They can be a heart scald."

"Will you have a drink?"

"No, thanks all the same." Seán tested one of the draught beers and called down to the cellar-man to put on an iron lung of Smithwicks.

"You will."

"I will not. I won't take a drink from an unemployed man. Wait till you get fixed up and then we'll see." He tested the pump again and gave a grunt of satisfaction.

"Nothing doing here I suppose?" Niall asked.

"'Fraid not. The boss had to let a barman go a few weeks back. They say the economy is booming. We don't see much signs of it around here."

"Any of the regulars know of anything?" Niall inquired.

"I'll ask around. But I doubt it. Most of them are in the same boat as yourself. On the dole and doing a few nixers here and there." With a plastic spatula Seán scooped the head off a freshly pulled pint, then topped it up.

Niall reckoned that the well-dressed types he'd seen going into the back room were hardly on the dole but it was too soon to ask about that. To the casual observer the pub certainly didn't look like the haunt of drug lords, but then again it could have been chosen for just that reason. It was unlikely that Gerry Connolly had got it wrong.

Seán went to serve a thin man who leant against the bar a few feet away from Niall.

"Any accidents today, Eamonn?" Seán asked with feigned sympathy.

"Cut it out, you."

Sean introduced him, adding, "There isn't a manhole in the city he hasn't had the misfortune of falling into. Even cracks in the pavement trip him up."

"Jasus, tell everyone why dontcha?" Eamonn said irritably. "Ruin a good racket."

"The Corpo are on to you. Another accident and you'll end up in the 'Joy. Anyway, Niall here is in the same boat."

"On the welfare?" Eamonn looked at him through bottle-end glasses one lug of which was repaired with electrical tape. "The country is fucked if you ask me. I blame the politicians, swanning around in helicopters and Mercedes, their hands out all the time for bribes. Fuck 'em all. You have to have a racket in this country nowadays to keep the wolf from the door. 'Course the big people get away with it with their accountants and lawyers and offshore deposits. The rest of us are only one jump ahead of the Guards." He took a huge swallow of stout; it was obviously not his first drink of the day. "And the Guards are tied up in their own scams. Second-hand motors, massage parlours, etc., etc. But they still have time to hassle the small man. Just a week ago they came in here and lifted Tommy Egan for an ATM scam. Imagine that, after we bailed out the bleeding banks. I ask you."

"Still, I reckon they're keen enough to get after the big-time villains." Niall hoped this might bring the conversation around to drug-trafficking and Stuke. It brought no response. "Knock that back and have another." When the new drinks arrived Niall suggested they sit down at a table. For some reason he felt that Eamonn might be more forthcoming out of earshot of Seán and a couple of others who leant against the bar.

A couple of pints later Niall said as casually as he could, "The fellas who use that room there don't seem to be short of a bob or two."

"You know about them?" Eamonn asked.

"I've heard a few things."

Eamonn took off his glasses and polished them with a well-used piece of chamois. The activity seemed to sober him up. Without the glasses he looked younger.

Niall decided to go for broke. "I wouldn't mind getting in on that racket. I've been around…"

"What racket is that?"

"Well, drugs…"

"Operating from where?" Eamonn held up the glasses, inspected them at close quarters and decided that they were clean enough.

"Here … maybe." Niall nodded in the direction of the closed door.

"Here? You've got your wires crossed, bud."

Even before this response Niall knew he'd blown it. Shortly afterwards Eamonn drained his glass and declined another drink even though it was well before closing time. He gathered up his newspaper and took his leave, banging the door after him.

Niall didn't sleep at all that night. His mind was in overdrive, churning through various options and possibilities, all of them ending in failure. Never too confident of his own ability and with only one week left, he began to panic.

That feeling undermined him the next day, which he wasted through indecision and by dividing his effort. He waited outside the diplomatic residence in Killiney at seven in the morning. There was just a chance Mark had spent the night there. It soon became clear that he hadn't. Niall drove back into town in the rush hour, wasting almost two hours, parked the car in Ranelagh village and explored every inch of Rathmines for most of the day, visiting shopping centres, pubs and amusement arcades. Then he drove back out to Killiney in the evening. And all for nothing; another day gone up in smoke. Was there something obvious that eluded him? The question formed and reformed in his overtired mind. He also knew that even if he got to meet Stuke, questions would be asked about background, ID and so on. Maybe the whole thing had been impossible from the word go.

Later that evening and against his better judgement, he called Gerry and briefly explained his predicament. Gerry didn't say much over the phone but some two hours later he turned up at the bedsitter.

"Christ, Niall," he took in the awful room, the damp spots and peeling plaster. "You're just not cut out for this. And you look tired."

Niall shrugged. He couldn't quite believe how good it was to see Gerry again, to have someone to talk to. He didn't realise how lonely he had been.

"You're going to go on with this?"

"Yes."

Gerry sat on the edge of the cot. "I spoke with Eamonn. That's why it took such a long…"

"What? You know him?"

"Slightly. I know his brother better." Gerry laughed. "Dublin isn't such a big place. Anyway, Eamonn clammed up because you came on a bit strong. Also you bought the drink and yet you were supposed to be down on your luck."

"He spotted that?"

"If Eamonn is anything like his brother he's smart enough. He may come across as a sort of harmless gombeen but … well, you know the type. He does jobs for Stuke by the way."

"No." In Niall's mind, Eamonn did not come anywhere near his image of a dealer.

"Oh yes. Falling down is just a sideline or a cover." Gerry grinned. "Maybe even an insurance policy. There's not much job security in working for Stuke."

"What does he do for him?"

"Distributes mainly. He's not a big player but he gets around." Gerry explained how local drug-pushers were often thrown out of different tenements by residents' associations. Usually when that happened Stuke would arrange for someone like Eamonn, a floater, to go into the area to keep the supply going and keep rival pushers out. Consequently, Eamonn was familiar with several different parts of the city where users gathered.

Was this at last the opening he so badly

needed? Niall wondered. He didn't want to get his hopes up and maybe Gerry's presence had something to do with it, but he felt more confident than he had in months.

"If you were interested he might take you along. For a consideration."

"That's OK. Cash isn't a problem."

"I had to tell him you weren't involved in the drug scene. That you were looking for someone, a user. But I didn't say any more than that."

"Thanks, Gerry. I wasn't getting anywhere on my own."

"Maybe you shouldn't take it any further. It's not too late to back out." Gerry went on to tell him about the risks, which were considerable. Stuke used his distributors like cannon fodder. If there was any trouble with the law or residents' associations it was the distributors who suffered. That was understood. No one involved Stuke. There could be trouble from rival gangs. Niall couldn't deny the feeling of fear that crawled through him but he wouldn't back down now. All his life he had been passive, never pushing the boat out. If he couldn't do this for Ros then he didn't deserve to live. It was that simple.

"You're probably wasting your time anyway," Gerry said slowly.

"Are you saying I still mightn't find him?"

"No, you may. But I don't think you'll do… anything." Gerry stood up and added quietly, "I've been there." He looked out the single window at the gathering dusk. "An operation they called it. I even had the excuse of following orders. But there isn't a day that passes when I don't regret it."

Niall was silent for a while and then said, "I have to find him."

"I know. Listen, get out of this rat-hole and come back to my place."

Niall thanked him for the offer but declined. They shook hands and Gerry touched him on the shoulder before facing into the rain.

He fell asleep from sheer exhaustion but awoke with a start at three in the morning. There was something on his mind. Rona! He had forgotten to call her. He threw on pants and shirt and went out to the landing. The public phone threw the usual tantrums but somehow he managed to get through.

"Niall, where have you been? I've been worried sick. The hotel said…"

"Sorry. I'm so sorry, Rona. I tried calling…"

"Where are you now?"

"I'm with Gerry." He gave her the number of his house. He would have to let Gerry know in the morning, to arm him with an excuse if she called.

"You're not there now."

"How do you mean?"

"Those pips. It's a coin box isn't it?"

"Yes. I don't want to… you know… run up his phone bill. I should have bought a cell phone." He wondered how many lies were necessary to support the first one.

"You could always offer to pay him…"

"So, is everything all right?" If she didn't accept the change of subject he had nothing to fall back on.

"Yes, and you?"

"Fine … You sound a bit down."

"Oh, some problems at work. I won't go into them now."

"Nothing too serious I hope. I'll be home soon. We can…"

"About another week?"

"Yes."

Despite the draught that blew up the staircase, Niall was damp with sweat when he got off the phone. Lying didn't come easily to him but that didn't deter him. For the first time ever he felt relieved to have ended a conversation with his wife. That feeling kept him awake for what remained of the night.

CHAPTER 23

EAMONN SQUIRRELLED AWAY the five hundred euro in a Nike hold-all and threw it into the back of the Nissan van.

"I'm taking a big risk," he said. "Stuke wouldn't take kindly to this little arrangement. You should've told me you knew Gerry Connolly. A decent skin according to the brother."

"He is."

"You must really want to find this fella." Eamonn gave him a canny look as if to assess whether there might be scope for a larger fee. A thousand had a nice round feel to it.

Niall nodded. He had already described him to Eamonn without success. He had no intention of going into the whys and wherefores.

"Yeah, he must be important to you." Eamonn prodded the thick glasses further up on his nose, fastened the seatbelt and put the van into gear.

Plunkett Mansions represented an experiment in social engineering in the eighties that went badly wrong. Tower blocks rose up out of a wasteland, the few open spaces were vandalised, and half-starved horses and ponies moved slowly over the ground, cropping what little grass they could find. The shrine to Saint Oliver Plunkett was smashed and covered in graffiti. On at least two walls Niall saw huge ads for solicitors who specialised in personal injury; free consultations were offered and promises of substantial damages.

"They shouldn't be allowed advertise," Eamonn said. "Too many gobshites getting into the game." He parked the van in an alley some distance away under a line of washing. "I sometimes feel like the ice-cream man." He grinned at Niall, revealing nicotine-stained, irregular teeth. It was true in a way; the appearance of the van seemed to change the current of life on the estate.

He led the way to a door that seemed to be boarded up like many of the others. It was deceptive, however, because the woodwork was hinged and gave at the first push. Inside what was once a small flat, a few addicts were already waiting in the gloom. The place stank of urine and toluene, and the floor was littered with old needles, bent spoons, cotton swabs and tie-ups. It was already fairly obvious to Niall that Mark would hardly come to this particular shooting gallery.

Eamonn asked one of the less strung out junkies to go outside on watch, promising to look after him later. How the word spread was unclear but over the next hour or so addicts appeared from nowhere with fistfuls of greasy notes. Many looked no more than fifteen or sixteen and some were in a bad way. There was one thirty-year-old on crutches. In an aside Eamonn explained that he had lost his leg to gangrene as a result of injecting dirty needles into his thigh, and then his groin when the veins ran out. He had full-blown Aids and was suffering from emphysema.

Every now and then Eamonn would go out and check with the man on watch. Most of the trade was in heroin but there was considerable demand for speed, benzedrine and ecstasy, the latter going to the youngest kids who were planning to go to raves.

One buyer didn't have the requisite amount of cash; he pleaded and cursed and almost became hysterical. Eamonn took what money he had and gave him a packet of diluted H. He reminded him that he would take methadone in part exchange and gave him the address of the dispensary in Pearse Street.

Some of them started to shoot up there and then, including a gaunt twenty-year-old who was HIV-positive.

"Hold it," Eamonn barked. "Wait till we're outta here." A few more deals and he was almost done. "Just one freebie and we're off."

He went outside, climbed a cement stairway to a third floor flat and pushed a packet of H through a letter box.

"There's an eejit doing cold turkey in there. This'll tempt him."

"Christ." Shocked by the earlier scenes, Niall felt sickened by this element of cold-blooded calculation.

"I don't make the rules. Anyway, they're all knackers."

Just then a woman stuck her head out a window and started to yell, "Fuck off youse! Mat! Mat! There's pushers here. Get Billy … Quick!"

Eamonn started to run and Niall followed him as best he could, almost falling down the last flight of steps. A beer bottle missed his head by inches. They made the van and took off on squealing tyres.

"Fucking vigilantes," Eamonn said when they were safely distant, "taking the law into their own hands. They'd beat the shit out of us if they had the chance."

With justification, Niall thought. When he recovered a degree of composure he asked where the users got the money from.

"Thieving, shoplifting, muggings, you name it." He jerked a thumb over a shoulder." I saw a few rent boys back there today. Christ, who'd touch them?"

"I didn't think it'd be so… bad." Niall could still see the eyes that stared out of the thin faces in that awful squat.

"Yeah, they're hooked all right," Eamonn said. "Those knackers never had anything going for them. You'd nearly be sorry for them at times." He sounded like a disinterested observer. "There was some talk a while back of the government making H cheaper and giving out free methadone."

"Wouldn't help your business."

"No, it'd fuck everything up. But it'll never

happen, thank god. The government hasn't the balls." He chuckled to himself. "No, we're safe enough. Stuke has a couple of politicians in his pocket anyway." He looked across at him. "Any sign of your friend back there?"

"No."

"I didn't think so. Well, we've two runs tomorrow, Seán McDermott Street and Ballyer."

Niall joined him for the morning run. Seán McDermott Street was an inner-city development and there was a possibility that Mark might show up there. After hanging around for well over an hour, experiencing the same human degradation as the day before, Niall gave up hope. He had those feelings of panic again. Because of Rona he couldn't really stay beyond the coming weekend; it wouldn't be fair to her. On the way back in the van he asked Eamonn if he knew where the better-off addicts now went to deal. It seemed that Gerry Connolly's hunch about Rathmines was wide of the mark, or at least behind the times. But it had got him a contact, and that was better than nothing.

"The snot noses move around a bit. There used to be a place near Rathmines Bridge. Coke mainly. But the Polis moved in on that patch. Then they moved to Temple Bar until the Polis put up security cameras at every street corner.

Lazy fuckers. They'd do anything rather than pound the beat."

"Where do they go now?" Niall interrupted. Eamonn's light-hearted approach to death-dealing began to get to him.

"I'm not sure. Stuke doesn't do much coke."

"Could you find out?"

Eamonn looked at him over the top of the bottle ends, made a sucking sound and a see-saw motion of the hand, "Risky."

"Well?"

"It'll cost." Eamonn cursed a Mazda driver who tried to pass him on the inside.

"OK."

"You must really want this punter."

"I may need a couple of other favours."

"Everything's available at a price." Eamonn grinned. He was on a winner here, the dream nixer. He might never need to fall again.

———

Kate relayed a message to her boss. "The ambassador would like you to drop into his office."

As he took the stairs to the top floor David wondered what lay behind this most unusual request. Since joining the embassy he hadn't once been invited into the inner sanctum.

The ambassador waved him to a Queen Anne chair and offered him a sherry; there were no other preliminaries. "It won't come as a surprise when I say that your posting here is not working out."

"Oh?" David raised an eyebrow. If His Excellency expected more of a reaction to this blunt opening gambit he was going to be disappointed.

"Yes, we're a small, lean outfit here and it's all hands on deck. The negotiating process involved in Brexit is extremely time-consuming as you may have gathered. I can't involve you in that work because it is not your forte. More importantly, from a diplomatic point of view it would be risky."

"I'm not sure I follow," David said disingenuously, careful not to make eye contact with the pompous ass who sat behind the carved desk. He concentrated on the plaster mouldings of the ceiling.

"I don't think any useful purpose would be served by going into details," the ambassador said and promptly went into considerable detail, concluding with the comment, "The Irish authorities can be quite sensitive. If they discovered the, am, particulars of your past, it could prove to be embarrassing all round and a hazard to navigation. The Irish-American connection, you see, among other things."

"So where does all this lead one?"

"I've asked Whitehall to transfer you. The point is there really isn't a job for you here. And we're too tight an operation to carry even one, am, passenger. It is affecting morale." He got up from his chair and sat on the desk facing him, hands interlocked across his paunch. Far from finding the encounter difficult, he seemed to be on a roll.

Now the avuncular bit, David thought. He knew, of course, that sooner or later it would come to this; nevertheless, he wasn't quite ready for the precise moment.

"If you want my advice," the ambassador said, "I think you should apply for early retirement. There's quite a good package, including an ex gratia award of five years' pension rights. If I were, am, holed below the water line I would certainly consider it very seriously. Yes, very seriously indeed."

"You would?"

"Yes."

David consulted his watch and left the room abruptly; he would not give him the satisfaction of a reaction and he certainly didn't wish to hear another nautical allusion. Back in his office he rang a contact in the Personnel Department of the Foreign Office and checked out the retirement package. It was not to be sneezed at; His Excellency had not been exaggerating. There was no time like the present; he began to clear out his desk, a chore which didn't take long, given the brevity of his stay. Even the filing press was virtually empty.

So his career was finally and officially over, but then it had been on hold for the last fifteen years. Apart from a certain self-pity which irritated him, he had no real regrets. After his wife's death in India he lost interest in most things; his will had sustained a wound that never healed. The only thing that bothered him about retirement was how he would cope without the structure of an office routine. He was conscious of his own predilections and lack of discipline. Still, he would manage all right, take up some hobby or other, perhaps sailing.

He called Mark and told him they were on the move again, this time to London, presumably for good. Mark seemed pleased.

CHAPTER 24

IT WAS AN ORDINARY afternoon in the city centre. Hordes of shoppers crossed against traffic lights, not even deigning to hurry since there was safety in numbers. Double-decker buses belched out exhaust fumes, hamburger cartons and other debris littered the footpaths. Buskers and religious proselytes worked different sections of the hurdy-gurdy boulevard.

Niall had done a couple of more runs with Eamonn the previous day but without success.

As he stood in the entrance of a slot machine arcade he wondered if Eamonn's advice could possibly be correct. It seemed unlikely that trafficking would be done in the very centre of O'Connell Street, unless there was something to be said for hiding in plain sight. Of course there was virtually no police presence and he had only seen one squad car in the hour and a half he had been waiting.

His attention was drawn to a youth, dressed in a denim jacket and tracksuit bottoms, who stood near the base of the spire. From time to time other youths slowed down as they passed by him. From his brief experience in the tenements, Niall could read the body language, the minimal eye contact, sleight-of-hand movements and the occasional gleam of tinfoil or plastic packets.

A stocky security man, dressed in black, asked him to move away from the arcade entrance. He crossed the street and took up a position in the doorway of a Burger King. Litter and dust swirled around his feet. Occasionally he looked into the restaurant as if waiting for a friend to come out, then he would re-direct his attention to the spire where, without doubt, business was being transacted. The fact that it was obvious to him made him worry in case others, possibly local shopkeepers, might report the matter. If that were to happen he would lose what was possibly his last chance of finding Mark.

A weak sun broke through the grey sky and shone into his face, obscuring his vision. He tried a different position further down the street but there were too many buses there which interfered with his line of sight. He moved back to Burger King and pulled the peaked cap further down to shade his eyes.

He peered into the restaurant again and caught, in a mirror or window, a reflection of a familiar figure. For a split second the shock of recognition made him think it was his own reflection. Almost in the same instant he noticed the lank dark hair and loping walk. He spun around and his blood began to race. As he watched the transaction everything seemed to slow down, the minute actions of contact, exchange, separation. Everything else was a blur. Then, suddenly, he couldn't see him any more. He started to run across the street, causing at least one car to swerve. When he made the other side he didn't know which direction to take. Out of some instinct he turned south, continuing to run. Crowds parted to let him through. His breath came in rasps. To his great relief, by the time he reached Clery's he'd picked up the trail again.

Now he had a new concern. What if Mark suddenly got into a car? There was no way Niall could get to his which he'd parked in Abbey Street. When they passed the turn for Abbey Street the die was cast; he would have to leave the car. He prayed that Mark would continue on foot.

Rain began to fall and many passers-by went into shops and restaurants for shelter. Mark buttoned his jacket and continued walking. Niall, who had been about thirty yards behind, had to let the gap widen because there were fewer people between them. On the other hand even if Mark did turn around it would be unlikely that he would recognise the man in the shabby, rain-soaked suit and cap.

He followed him around the giant rib-cage of College Green, past Trinity and into Grafton Street. The rain stopped and the buskers and pavement artists came out from shelter. To his amazement, Mark stopped to listen to a youth playing a carpenter's saw with a violin bow. A small crowd formed around him and an enterprising Traveller kid worked the crowd with a polystyrene cup, pretending he was part of the act. Mark put a coin into the cup and walked on.

They passed the College of Surgeons and

continued into Harcourt Street where a plethora of small hotels provided token accommodation in exchange for liquor licenses. This street was about half way between Rathmines and the city centre. Mark turned and went up a few steps to the door of a redbrick house. He fumbled for a key, opened the door and went in. Niall waited outside until he saw a light come on in a front window on the fourth floor. He had the exact coordinates. At last he had run him to ground. At last. He felt as if a gift had been bestowed on him.

Now, however, was not the time, and he needed to contact Eamonn once more for certain items. He walked back to Abbey Street to pick up the car; his breathing became easier.

He drove around the city for a while, deciding on his next move for the following day. There was no point in dithering; only action mattered. Without fully realising it, he found himself on the Western Bypass and recognised some of the terrain that hadn't yet been developed. Maybe it was that recognition or some deeper instinct that lured him further out.

The village of Maynooth was much as he remembered it: ivy-covered houses, intimate pubs – some at the back of grocery shops – narrow streets and dry-stone walls. And at one end the barrack-like seminary, now a full university. He parked just inside the gates and walked around the grounds. He recalled a line his Biblical Studies master used to quote, 'Then shall the manslayer return and go into his old city and house from whence he fled'.

He could even identify the window of the room he once inhabited. Looking out of that window so many years ago one of his friends had said, "There's no peace out there, Niall. No peace." But those were the days when it was good to be a priest; when the faith was strong and the purveyors of that faith were in good standing. He wondered how many of his friends had real vocations. Some joined up for status or security reasons, others for their mother's sake, still others for the simple reason that they would not inherit the farm or any part of it. Of course many were sincere but, like Niall, they tended to worry about mixed motives and doubts. The system did not appreciate doubters and it gave short shrift to healthy questioning. There was a fair amount of primitive spin-doctoring and, with hindsight, one could almost say there was an element of brainwashing in the harsh discipline, the emphasis on submission and the constant repetition of prayers.

So in the end he had opted for doubt rather than comfortable certainty. And that choice had given him a wife, a daughter, a family, human love, so many other choices along the way and now the final one. 'Before his days be full, he who conceived sorrow shall perish'. Did that apply to Mark or himself? One had already conceived sorrow, the other was now prepared to do so. If both were to perish, so be it. The seminary and the memory of what went on inside those walls offered no alternative and no peace. The curriculum had been heavily influenced by the punishing god of the Old Testament with little reference to the love of Jesus Christ and the New Covenant.

Without question it was Ros who had given him life, so Mark had killed both of them. If justice was the price of his soul Niall was prepared to pay it. He walked back to the car and left the grey, brooding building behind him for the last time.

They mean well. This was the phrase Rona kept repeating to herself. She'd enjoyed the golf game and had played well up to her handicap. It was good to be out in the fresh air for almost half a day before winter closed in. But she couldn't quite shrug off the feeling that Betty and Si, despite their kindness, were treating her as a project. They had suggested the game and insisted that she join them for dinner in the clubhouse.

"How is the melon?" Betty inquired with a smile.

"Fine thanks. Fresh." That's what one said about melon or any fruit starter.

"I think the salmon is farmed." Si furrowed his brow and chewed pensively, his head to one side. "Didn't they say it was wild, Bets?"

"They did indeed, Snookums. But they didn't know they were dealing with a man of such refined taste buds."

"Well it is my business," Si said, a little miffed, drawing a napkin across his mouth. "If I tried that on with my discerning clients I'd soon hear all about it."

"I couldn't tell the difference. Could you, Rona?"

"What difference?"

"Between wild and farmed salmon."

"I don't think so." Now they were roping her into their little games. No, that was unfair. Yet, somehow, she felt like a widow taken out and entertained on sufferance. Christ, what was getting into her? The job or rather the non-job? Hardly. All of that seemed so insignificant compared with the tragedy, the fact that she was, what, an orphan? It was strange that there was no word to describe a parent who lost a child. She wished Niall would get back soon. She'd spoken twice to Gerry Connolly and on both occasions Niall was out. It was very odd but at least he was hardly out painting the town red.

"… I was perfectly entitled to a free drop-out on the tenth," Si was saying. "My ball had plugged in a divot hole. No penalty. Isn't that right, Rona?"

"I think so. You know the rules better than I do." She forced a smile. With a headache coming on she struggled through the main course and coffee. Several times she resisted the temptation to say she was tired and needed to go home. At Betty's insistence they arranged another outing for the following week; Niall would be back then and would make up the fourth.

When she eventually made the sanctuary of her home she swallowed two aspirin and went to bed. Niall would be home soon but, as always before sleeping, her last thought was that she would never see Ros again.

CHAPTER 25

IT WAS RAINING as Niall walked from Rathmines to Harcourt Street. The rain was being driven towards him and he had to pause occasionally to wipe his spectacles. The north wind seemed to get inside him and freeze his blood.

There was no difficulty about getting into the building; he simply waited on the top step until a tenant came out, then he slipped through the hall door before she closed it. He went up the gloomy staircase to the third floor and selected what he deemed to be the right flat. There was no light coming from under the door but he waited for a while, listening intently. A man passed him on the landing and paid him no attention. Niall began to work on the lock with a cold steel chisel. Despite the poor condition of the lock and surrounding woodwork he made slow progress. Beads of sweat appeared on his forehead and re-appeared as soon as he wiped them off.

The thought of failure made him panic but also gave him added strength. After one desperate heave he heard the woodwork begin to splinter. A little later he was able to open the door. Before going into the room he did what he could to disguise the damage. Then he felt a sharp pain in his left hand and realised that a splinter had pierced the palm. He quickly wrapped his handkerchief around it, hoping that no blood had dripped on to the floor.

He closed the door quietly behind him and switched on the lights briefly to find his bearings. An old parka jacket hanging on a hook on the back of the door confirmed that this was Mark's flat. He went quickly to the single window and pulled down the blind. The flat was nothing more than a single room with an old gas cooker in one corner screened off by a plastic curtain.

Niall explored the shelves in the kitchen area, placed the briefcase on a work surface and clicked the catches. The oven door was open and emitted a sickening smell of burnt fat. The only other sign that someone had used the facilities was a saucepan which contained the congealed remnants of baked beans.

When he emerged from the kitchen area he positioned a straight-backed chair directly in front of the door, sat down and began a long wait. Several times during the vigil his will faltered and he fought to regain his focus.

He could hear the traffic pass by on the wet main street, the rain on the roof – it sounded like hail – and the wind whistling down the chimney, rustling the empty crisp packets and other debris that filled the fire grate. There were moments when he couldn't believe the reason he was here, nor could he predict the outcome; at other times the logic was unassailable and the result almost predestined. He kept the briefcase on his knees and checked the contents periodically.

The headlights of the traffic on Harcourt Street shone through the thin blind and made ghostly patterns on the ceiling. Almost one hour had passed already. He walked across the bare floorboards to the window and again consulted his watch in a shaft of light from the street. Almost one a.m. He went back to the chair and sat down again. He was calm now, calmer than he could have imagined. The visit to Maynooth had, if anything, strengthened his resolve.

Perhaps another hour passed. Then he heard footsteps – slow, steady ones – on the stairs, followed by sounds of a key scratching around a lock. He hoped the damaged woodwork would not scare Mark away.

The Jackson Pollock might look better on the wall opposite the south-facing window, Lorna Baldwin thought. She was redesigning her new office in her mind, which teemed with ideas. The spacious and well-appointed office was a tangible symbol of her success. Though ambitious, she hadn't really expected to become the senior fashion buyer at such a young age, but the element of surprise made it all the more enjoyable. And if she handled her new responsibilities well she would have a shot at a vice presidency at least. Everything was set fair.

"Enjoy." Rona laid her gift of African violets

on the desk.

Caught off guard for an instant, Lorna looked startled. "Thanks, they're lovely. Sorry, I've been sort of daydreaming."

"I remember that feeling." It was at least two decades ago when Rona got her break and she had set about personalising her office. She could not have imagined back then that she would be kicked upstairs in her late forties when she still had so much to offer. Still, she had recovered from the shock and didn't feel bitter about it. In fact Lorna seemed OK and she was sure they'd got along.

"I'm looking forward to working with you," Lorna said as if on cue.

"Me too."

"I've always respected your judgement."

"Thanks. But I've made a few mistakes in my time, I can tell you."

"Too few to mention."

Rona laughed. "I'm not so sure. But I think I learnt from them and you might be interested in having this." She held out a well-stuffed, loose-leaf file. "I've documented most of the hazards of the job, the banana skins you never see, the false economies. There are also some notes on suppliers, their mark-ups and negotiating strategies."

"That will be a great help, Rona. Thank you."

They spent some time talking about fashion, how the best designers always stressed the importance of cut and fabric and how real style somehow emerged only when those two essential elements were present.

When Rona left, Lorna spent five minutes leafing through the file before she binned it. She was going to do the job her own way.

The thinning trees of Virginia scrolled over the windscreen as Rona drove home. Autumn was well established now and the evenings were drawing in. One advantage of her new advisory role was that she could keep more regular office hours and avoid those late sessions which in the past meant that she rarely saw daylight during the winter months.

There was still an orange glow in the sky and as she drove she had the strangest feeling that Ros could have been sitting beside her in the passenger seat. It wasn't a hallucination or an epiphany, simply a feeling of closeness. They could have been having one of their many conversations about events on Capitol Hill, low standards in high places, popular music – Rona had always tried to keep up – those strange TV talk shows that encouraged people to punch the daylights out of each other. There never had been any boundaries or taboo subjects, even during puberty when Niall did his best to assume, for his daughter's sake, that boys didn't exist.

Rona found herself smiling. For some reason the absence of her daughter's physical presence no longer terrified her. Ros had lived. She had created an aura, a sphere of influence that touched many people. Her spirit could not be extinguished.

A distant acquaintance passed by and honked. Rona waved in recognition; the smile lingered on her face for a long while. And Niall would be back soon.

―――――――

When the light went on Mark blinked and shook his head as if trying to clear it. He looked at Niall in mild surprise but little comprehension.

"You know why I'm here?" Niall stood up and held the back of the chair.

"No … not more photos and stuff. Does my old man … did he send…?" He was disoriented, coming off a high. His eyes were filmy, the pupils pinned.

"Yes. I met him. He wants you to tell me the truth. Face to face."

"Truth about what? I don't…" He swayed slightly and recovered his balance. "Jesus, I miss…"

"Who do you miss?"

"The States… better there, you know, easier …What are you doing here?" He scratched his face and neck. Awkwardly, like a reflex action that was mistimed, he drew the kitchen curtain aside, then let it fall back.

"Sit down. It's time we had a serious talk."

Mark sat on the edge of the bed and continued to fidget, his hands clawing at imaginary cobwebs. "Talk about what…?"

"About Ros. What you did to her. Why did you have to kill her?" Niall placed the chair nearer the bed and sat, craning forward. His senses were so honed the sounds of rain on glass were like drum beats.

"Kill…? No, no, you're wrong." He swallowed several times in quick succession. His lips and throat were parched. "An accident … unfortunate…"

"Unfortunate?" Coming from Mark, the word was an obscenity. Niall remembered all too clearly the car wreck which bore the signs of having been viciously and repeatedly rammed by a much heavier vehicle.

"If it makes it easier for you to talk why don't you take something? I don't mind. I'm not a killjoy like your old man." But Niall didn't want to talk anymore; there was no need.

Mark gave him a look of canny appraisal. "I'm not afraid…" he got up and went behind the plastic curtain.

"Take your time." Niall moved his chair slightly to keep him in his line of sight.

When mark re-emerged he was rolling down a shirt sleeve. "I'd offer you coffee only I've run out."

"Oh, there's no need for that. I know what it's like to be on your own in a place like this. I was born here in this town. A long time ago. So this is a kind of nostalgia trip for me." His eyes never left Mark's face. "Well, you're too young to appreciate that feeling…"

"Yeah."

"I think he was right, whoever said, 'you can't go back'."

"London in a couple of days … On the move again. Anywhere … better than here."

"But you'll hardly remember London. So for you it'll be a new experience. Not for David, of course. He'll remember it and will be able to make comparisons with other places. That's the great benefit of travel. Comparisons, contrasts…"

"Travel…" Mark's eyes rolled and his mouth was slightly curved in a trance-like smile.

"You're feeling better now?"

"Better." Mark lay back on the bed, breathing gently. His cowled eyes started to close.

Niall reached down and quietly brought the briefcase more readily to hand. He watched Mark all the time and noticed that a fleck of foam had appeared at the corner of his mouth. He stood over the sleeping face, waited a while, then quietly went behind the curtain. The needle was on a shelf in full view. He opened a cupboard door and looked into the coffee jar where he had earlier found the stash – and added to it the stuff Eamonn had provided. The jar was almost empty. Maybe he wouldn't need the syringe in the briefcase.

When he returned to the bed he saw that the inane smile had gone from the sleeping face and that Mark's breathing was more laboured. He pulled the window blind further down to eliminate a chink of light at the bottom, and waved away a moth that circled over the prone body. Mark groaned a couple of times, tried to sit up and fell back. Sounds of scuffling came from the landing outside the door. Niall stood frozen, hardly daring to breathe. Gradually the sounds subsided; he sat down weakly.

Sweat glazed Mark's forehead; his face was contorted. He tried to sit up again but failed; he twisted on to his side, his knees drawn up under him. No position seemed to provide comfort and the groans that escaped his throat were weaker now. His eyelids fluttered, giving glimpses of eyes that were jaundiced and without expression. Without meaning to, Niall traced the sign of the cross on the sweating forehead and began to pray, *"Miseratur tui omnipotens Deus, et dimissis peccatis tuis, perducat te ad vitam aeternum."* Mark's body convulsed several times, went rigid, then relaxed. A long breath like a sigh came from his mouth.

Niall continued to wait, then he leant forward and touched the tips of his fingers to Mark's neck; there was no pulse. He tried not to remember that this was the kid who used to play with saucepan lids on the floor of his kitchen. Trembling, he got to his feet. Some words from the sacrament of extreme unction formed on his lips. His body was bathed in sweat. He retrieved the briefcase and switched off the light. As he opened the door he looked back once at the lifeless, shadowy figure. He went out. It was three-thirty in the morning. He walked quickly, this time with the rain on his back, and as he passed over Rathmines Bridge he threw the back-up syringe into the canal.

When he reached his own building he phoned the police on their confidential line and pretended he was a neighbour, concerned about a young man who might have odeed. He gave Mark's address in Harcourt Street, but rang off before the police could question him further. That was the most he could do to ensure that the body was discovered sooner rather than later. Presumably, that was also the motivation behind David's call to the police in Virginia on that awful night eight months ago when Ros was killed.

It was over. He had achieved what he had planned almost from day one. There was no elation or depression, but he was still keyed up and sleep was out of the question. To keep himself occupied he packed his bags. There was no need to tell Gerry he was leaving; he would find out in time. As would David, and he would probably come to the conclusion that it was an accidental overdose, although it didn't really matter what he thought.

When his bags were packed he called a taxi and waited in the room for it to arrive. On the way to the airport he caught a glimpse of the taxi man's newspaper. Bombs had gone off at various points along the new customs border with

Northern Ireland. The taxi man believed that the Peace Agreement was now in tatters and that the 'Troubles' were about to begin all over again – and this time there was no one in the White House with the will or ability to broker a new deal. The damage that was being caused by Brexit was incalculable.

Later that morning Niall was on a plane to New York, but this time he wasn't emigrating; he was going home. Though on the verge of exhaustion he was too pumped to sleep or relax. He was excited at the prospect of meeting Rona and this kept him awake all the way to Kennedy. When they brought the duty-free trolley around he had the presence of mind to buy some perfume for her. During the taxi ride to La Guardia he nodded off for a few minutes at a time, coming to with a jerk and a sense of indefinable shock.

"Rough journey?" the cabbie queried on one occasion, looking at him through the rearview mirror.

"Rough enough." Given all of the sleepless nights, he was carrying a huge sleep deficit.

In the departure lounge at La Guardia he dozed off and missed one shuttle but got on the next one. It was just as well he hadn't given Rona his flight times. There was a long queue for taxis at Reagan but he eventually got one and they headed for Virginia. It was mid-afternoon when he walked through his own front door, marvelling at the luxury of his home. He made coffee and drank two cups in quick succession. Then he went for a hot bath which acted like a poultice, drawing out fatigue toxins through every pore. He completed this ritual with a cold shower, a shave and a brisk towelling down.

He decided not to call Rona at work, but to surprise her when she came home in about two hours' time. To enhance the surprise he set the table for dinner, put the perfume beside her placemat and phoned for a Chinese take-away.

Unfortunately, he was fast asleep in an armchair when she came through the door. She hugged him and called his name until he came to.

"Aw, damn. I wanted to surprise you."

"You did," she said laughing. "I'm glad you're back." She kissed him on the forehead.

"Me too."

She stood back, appraising him. "You look tired."

"They have tee-shirts over there saying, 'I survived Ireland for a whole day'. So I guess I did all right."

"A good time? Did you cover all the bases?"

"And how. Gerry Connolly was kindness itself. I couldn't have … covered half the ground without him. He was just great."

"You were out the couple of times I tried his number."

"He told me. I must've just missed you on both occasions. I really should get a cell phone. Ros used to call me a dinosaur, remember?"

"I do remember."

"So, what about these problems at work?"

They sat down to dinner and she told him about her new advisory position which she described with some exaggeration as death by a thousand cuts. He told her there was nothing wrong with being an elder statesman or mentor, tossing the odd bit of advice to the striving young Turks. To his mind this back-room role was far preferable to being at the coalface. It didn't mean she was becoming a supernumerary; if Bloomingdales thought that they would fire her, which they obviously didn't want to do. As they chatted he helped convince her that there were actually many advantages, not least the fact that she would have more leisure time.

"Yes," he said heartily, "more time to look after me."

"What about me?"

"You'll have more time to look after yourself as well."

"Hardy har. What got into you over there?" She put her hand on his and smiled at him, the man she would gladly grow old with. Now that he was back she saw things in a better light. Even a condo in Florida didn't seem like such a mind-numbing cliché. They went to bed early, made love and continued to chat long into the night.

Niall's re-entry into the workplace was equally smooth. The staff seemed glad to have him back after his three-week absence. They tended to look to him for leadership since Jack Wyndham was still stumbling from one indecision to another and back again. During his first few days back in harness Niall rescued two valuable contracts that had all but been lost due to Jack's vacillation, and he convinced one of the rising young surveyors not to leave the firm. Niall went about his work quietly but it seemed to be the quietness of someone who didn't need to raise his voice to be heard. He didn't rush into things but sifted the evidence carefully and came to reasoned decisions. He was more relaxed at meetings than he'd ever been and stated his case with gravitas and sometimes a little wit. Norbert made another attempt to head-hunt him and though Niall had no intention of changing jobs, he was flattered by the man's persistence.

Having him back, and renewed, helped Rona re-establish the close friendships that had come under strain while he was away. They brought Betty and Si out to dinner one evening and had a pleasant and carefree time. Si had hired a new chef who was working out well and, as yet, had shown no signs of being a sex maniac. Business was booming and he had satisfied the IRS about his tax affairs. The subject of the Highsmith's came up a couple of times and there was no question of treating it as taboo. To Rona's relief the conversation wasn't forced and she didn't have the sense that special efforts were being made to lighten the atmosphere or spare her feelings.

Getting back to normal was not all plain sailing, however, because it left them vulnerable to the feeling that all was well, a state of mind that was easily shattered when they thought of their loss. Since they did not want to avoid memories of their daughter they had no choice but to suffer these frequent and painful reverses. Although Rona was better able to handle these situations, Niall was making great strides.

His anger had subsided and he was vaguely surprised that it had not been replaced by guilt, or by fear of reprisal, real or imagined. Since he was still grieving maybe there was no room for such feelings. Besides, he had done what had to be done, no more and no less; it had not been a discretionary act. Doubtless, the Church would see it as a sinful act or a 'grave moral disorder' to use the modern parlance, but then the Church did not, under Canon Law, regard paedophilia as a sin; it was a psychological aberration which meant that sinful motivation could not be imputed. Some logic. On a few occasions he had considered going to confession but quickly abandoned the idea, since absolution was granted only where genuine contrition was involved, and in his heart's core he didn't have anything to be contrite about.

One morning he brought the dog for a walk before breakfast. Hamm was getting a little old but he still enjoyed a run in the woods and never tired of chasing and retrieving a stick. When they got back to the house Niall removed the collar and leash and hung them up on the hall stand.

"Anything wrong?" He thought Rona seemed upset.

"See for yourself." She waved vaguely in the direction of a letter that lay on an end table. He brought it to the light of the bay window, put on his glasses, and read,

'Rona and Niall,

Mark died early on Thursday morning, R.I.P.

The police were called to his flat in Harcourt Street and found him dead. He had overdosed on contaminated heroin. That was the official verdict at least.

David Highsmith.'

He laid the letter aside and waited on tenterhooks for Rona to say something. She maintained a stolid silence.

"I can't say I'm surprised or upset..." he began.

"The stamp is Irish and the postmark is Dublin ... I checked on the internet..."

"So?"

"You knew that David had been posted there. You knew it all the time." Her voice began to tremble.

"Rona, what...?"

"You planned it. You followed him over

there … tracked him down and … killed him." She could scarcely believe the words that had come from her mouth. But Niall's strange behaviour while he was away and the tone of the letter were more than circumstantial.

"Yes," he said quietly. "I didn't want you to know. I thought there would be guilt but there isn't. There isn't."

"You're a murderer…" She got the word out but couldn't go on.

"Yes."

"You admit it?" Her eyes widened; fear wasn't far away. She leant against a wall for support.

"I killed him with just cause. If that makes me a murderer so be it." He had reconciled himself to that a long time ago. Justifiable homicide might be a better term for the deed but there was no equivalent term for the perpetrator of such a deed.

"My god, how can you live with that?"

"Because whatever pain results from it will be less than before. Even if it were greater I would gladly suffer it. I did what had to be done, Rona. And I would do it again." His face was ghostlike in its pallor but he spoke calmly with the assurance of someone who had spent many long nights going over the ground.

"What have you become…?" She tried to look at him but could not bring herself to do so. How could love for his daughter, even an excess of love, have driven him to this?

"Rona, I haven't changed. It was in me all the time."

"You took the law into … the moral law…" She broke down. This was Niall, the man she'd lived with for almost twenty-five years.

"The law failed us."

"And god…?"

Niall didn't hesitate. "What god?"

She sat down and rocked from side to side, holding her head. Tears ran between her fingers. The light from the window had begun to fade as dusk closed in. Street lights came on, one of them just outside the Highsmith house now rented by a retired couple. Hamm, the spaniel, snored in his basket in the kitchen. On waking he would probably go down the corridor to lie outside Ros's bedroom door.

Niall lay awake for most of the night listening to Rona's sobbing from the spare room, and when morning came he heard her storm out of the house and the angry revs of her car.

Later on he phoned her office to discover she had not been in. Just before lunchtime there was a message from her on his answering machine saying that she had to go away. There was no reason given, no destination and no return date. With sinking heart he wondered if this finally was the retribution he'd feared, losing the second woman in his life. It was likely that David's letter had been designed to bring this about. Would it have made any difference if he had confided in Rona before he'd gone to Dublin?

Why had he not done so? To shield her or to give himself more room for manoeuvre? He had no clear answers, only a burning sensation in the pit of his stomach and a feeling that the final cost of justice might be far higher than he'd realised. However high it proved to be, he would pay it.

Rona had driven about half-way towards her parents' home in Philadelphia when she pulled over to the hard shoulder just outside the Baltimore tunnel. Her eyes were sore from crying and lack of sleep. She realised that she couldn't put her elderly parents through all the torment again. Besides, how could they possibly advise her? She had also ruled out her therapy group, and Betty, for different, though equally compelling, reasons. And Father Matos would be a waste of time; a practical man, he was more interested in renovating church buildings than dealing with questions of conscience. It occurred to her, not for the first time, that when the chips were down there was no one to turn to. For years she had depended on, and was influenced by, Niall's moral sense but that was no longer available to her. How had he changed so radically? Or had he always got this hidden layer buried deep in his nature?

She took the next off ramp and drove for a long time with no particular destination in mind.

Because she was overwrought her driving was erratic and on more than one occasion she changed lanes without meaning to. Once, she hit the median and for a few seconds the car went out of control on the greasy surface of the road.

Niall could understand her need to get away. She was undoubtedly shocked by what had happened, whereas he had plenty of time to come to terms with the deed which, in any case, he regarded as inevitable. As well as that, the manner of the revelation – the curt letter from David – had obviously shaken her badly. She had never walked out on him before and he knew that she had not done so lightly. Her distress bothered him and made him feel queasy.

He made calls to Betty and to a member of Rona's therapy group whom he knew slightly. He tried to make light of the calls, pretending that he might have misinterpreted an arrangement they'd made. It became clear that she had not contacted them. His worry deepened.

He rang her parents' home and spoke with her mother on the pretext of getting together for Thanksgiving. When she asked to speak with Rona he knew that she hadn't gone there. So where had she gone and what was her state of mind?

There was no point in contacting the police;

she would not yet be classed as a missing person. Besides, he had no faith in the police. He shouldn't have been so blunt with her but she had confronted him and he couldn't very well lie to her. If he now regretted what he'd done in Dublin it was only because of its effect on his kind and sensitive wife. She had suffered more than enough already.

With nothing left to do at least for the time being, he busied himself in the garden, tending rose bushes and flower beds, hoping she would return, though acutely aware that he had no reason to justify such hope.

At the back of her mind Rona realised that she was in no condition to drive. Her reflexes were slow and tears clouded her vision. She was a hazard to herself and other road-users. When she saw a sign for a Holiday Inn she pulled off the road and checked into the hotel.

Not wishing to be completely on her own, she stayed late in the lobby watching TV with some other sleepless residents who had come down from their rooms to be with other people. There was professional wrestling and then a couple of back-to-back late-night chat shows. The manic idiocy of the programmes served as a distraction which in turn had a calming effect on her.

A few minutes into a black-and-white movie she was fast asleep in the armchair. It was a deep sleep and though she woke around five she felt fairly rested. There was no point in going to bed at that hour but she went to her room and had a shower. Then she had a cup of coffee in the dining room and paid her bill. Outside, it was cold and dry. The pensive mood of early morning had always appealed to her.

She drove, slowly at first, until her confidence returned. There was little traffic on the road at that hour and there seemed to be a kind of fellow feeling between the few drivers who passed by. The sky was like white veined marble with a barely perceptible orange glow to the east. Largely out of habit she followed the Beltway towards Virginia but had no definite plan. The headquarters of the giant corporations that ringed Washington seemed deserted, though many of them were lighted inside, possibly for security reasons. The lights were wan and sickly against the dawn. She used to wonder what influence those giant corporations had on the political process; they certainly didn't locate around the Washington Beltway for the view.

Without fully realising why, she took the next off-ramp and after twenty minutes or so found herself in the vicinity of St. John's Cemetery where Ros was buried. She followed her instincts by parking the car and walking through the gates.

At the graveside she noticed the flowers that

Niall must have left at some time in the last few days. Sitting on the grass in front of the headstone, she began to commune wordlessly with her daughter as she had done in the months since the accident. She realised that of all her friends and relatives, Ros alone had the honesty and common-sense she so badly needed. She should have come here first instead of driving aimlessly on the highways in a state of confusion. A light rain began to fall and turned the cypress trees dark olive. She looked up at the changing sky so that the rain washed her face and ran into her eyes and mouth. Her anxieties seeped into the damp earth and she grew in acceptance; an unaccustomed sense of peace enfolded her. Ros would not have condoned what Niall had done but, knowing his heart, would she have forgiven him?

When she returned to the house she saw him at the end of the garden, his thin frame soaked to the skin. He was weeding between the rose bushes, oblivious of the rain. He sensed her presence, looked up in hope and gratitude; he wiped the moisture from his glasses. As she approached him he let the garden hoe fall and walked towards her, diffidently at first, and then with quickening pace.